VALENTINE KISSES AT THE STABLES ON MUDDYPUDDLE LANE

Heart-warming, uplifting romance

Etti Summers

CHAPTER ONE

October Rees eyed the man standing in front of her on this cold and dark January morning with trepidation. She'd met him during her job interview the other day, and she didn't think he liked her much.

Looking at him now, she was even more convinced she was right. In his mid-to-late forties, Nathan Windrush was the stables' general manager and was going to be her immediate boss, although it had been Petra, the woman who owned the stables, who had asked most of the questions. October had a feeling he was going to be a hard taskmaster, and it didn't help that she got the impression he was suspicious of her reasons for applying for the position of groom, since her previous job had been in a prestigious showjumping yard.

But she was here now, and both she and Nathan had to make the best of it.

'Hi,' she said, and Nathan nodded at her, his expression wary. He had been dour at the interview, hardly saying anything, and she'd felt the weight of his assessing gaze throughout.

She felt it again this morning and she hoped he'd leave her alone to get on with things, because she didn't think she'd be able to cope if he didn't. As an experienced groom, October knew what she was doing, but she also realised that she'd have to prove herself, and that she might have to get used to him looking over her shoulder for a while until she did.

His breath steamed around his head in the early morning chill, and the glow of the yard lights cast shadows across his face. He had a short stubbly beard, and a bobble hat pulled firmly down around his ears. An ancient waxed jacket, faded jeans and a pair of steel-toecap boots completed the picture, and October felt overdressed in her clean black breeches, Barbour boots (they looked like wellies but smarter), and padded jacket. Underneath, she wore a Joules fleece, and beneath that she was wearing a long-sleeved tee shirt and a pullover. On bitterly cold winter days it was better to wear too much than too little, and October operated on the premised that if she got too warm, she could always take something off, but if she got too cold and she didn't have any other layers to put on, she was going to freeze.

'If I tell you what's what for today, I'll leave you to get on with it,' Nathan said. 'Charity is working this morning and so is Petra. Charity stables her horse here in exchange for labour,' he added, 'so she knows the ropes. If you're unsure of anything and I'm not around, ask her.

There's a whiteboard in the office with jobs on, so if you're at a loose end take a look at that.'

October nodded; she'd spotted the whiteboard at her interview. The tasks were roughly divided into three columns – today, this week, and whenever. The "whenever" heading had made her smile.

Nathan continued, 'We turn the horses out every morning, no matter what the weather, and they all come in at night. I'll be down to the fields in a minute with some silage for them, so if you want to carry on taking those ponies there—' he jerked his head at the row of looseboxes to his left '—I'll start on this lot. Oh, and you'll find a pair of Shetlands in one stall: keep them together because they'll pine if they're apart. And the donkey can go into the same field as the Shetlands.'

October loved donkeys and she couldn't wait to meet this one. There was something very appealing about their long ears and scruffy coats.

Once the assorted equines had been turned out into the fields to graze, October diligently mucked out each stall and re-laid it with fresh bedding. She didn't mind the hard work – she'd been mucking out since she was a tot and she enjoyed the exercise – but she was grateful that Charity was there, so she didn't have to do it all by herself.

Towards the end of preparing the first stall, she had taken her jacket off. During the second she'd removed her fleece, and now she was working in just a tee shirt and a pullover. It was heavy work forking soiled straw into a barrow then hauling it to the manure pile, and it certainly got her heart pumping.

'Fancy a hot drink and a warm in the kitchen?' Charity suggested when the mucking out was done.

She was younger than October, but only by about five or so years, and she'd explained that her horse was the pretty mare called Storm, and that she'd been riding at the stables since she was a teenager.

There had been a bit of a sticky moment when the girl had asked what had brought her to the stables on Muddypuddle Lane, but October had evaded the question by airily saying, 'My mother lives in Picklewick so I'm spending some time with her.'

It wasn't strictly a lie, although it was very close to one. October hadn't come to the village for the sole purpose of spending time with her mother (although it was lovely seeing more of her). October had moved in with Lena because she didn't have anywhere else to go. The showjumping yard where she had previously worked had provided living accommodation as part of her employment, so when she'd left she'd effectively become homeless.

Lena was delighted to have her back, especially since October's grandma had moved into a care home recently. Her grandma had lived with her mum, and Lena had told October she felt as though she was rattling around in the house on her own since, so she welcomed the company.

October felt a little despondent about having to move back in with her mum. When she'd left home ten years ago, she'd had big plans and driving ambition, but none of it had come to fruition. However, it was nice being fussed over and having meals cooked for her for a change; although she did try to do her fair share of the chores, and she loved spending more time with her mother.

Feeling unaccountably nervous, October followed Charity into the house, where a wall of warm air hit her. Her cheeks reddened in the sudden heat, and she hastily took her jumper off.

The kitchen was redolent with the smell of coffee and baking bread, with a slight undertone of dog and horse. Two dogs were cuddled together on an armchair and both raised their heads when she came in, their tails thumping on the cushions. One was a black spaniel and the other was a white Jack Russell terrier with a blob of brown over one eye.

Nathan was already there, his hands curled around a mug, and when he saw October looking at the dogs he said, 'The black one is Queenie, she's Petra's, and the Jack Russell is mine. His name is Patch. They've got more sense than to be out on a day like today.'

An elderly man had his back to the room, but he turned around at the sound of Nathan's voice. 'Hello, you must be October. I'm Amos, and I own the stables.'

October blinked: she had been under the impression that Petra was the owner. 'Nice to meet you,' she said, trying to work out the dynamics.

Amos must have realised she was confused because he added, 'I might own the stables, but Petra runs it. She's my niece.' He opened the oven door and a waft of steam billowed out. Bending down, he carefully lifted out a loaf of golden-crusted bread and October's tummy rumbled.

'Tea or coffee?' Charity asked her, heading over to the kettle.

'Coffee, please. Strong. No milk.'

'How about you, Petra? Would you like a coffee?'

Out of the corner of her eye, October noticed Petra shudder. 'No thanks. I think I'll have tea,' the woman said, and

October saw Nathan shoot her a concerned look.

Someone's mobile tinkled into life and Nathan patted his pocket before drawing out a phone. When he looked at the screen his whole face was transformed as he smiled widely, and his eyes lit up.

'I take it that must be Megan,' Petra said, accepting a mug of hot tea from Charity.

Charity handed another mug to October, who took it and sipped it gratefully. 'Thank you.'

Charity smiled. 'You're welcome.'

'Aw, look at him,' Petra chortled, her eyes on Nathan. 'He's gone all bashful.'

Bashful wasn't a word October would associate with Nathan, but he did look a little sheepish.

He glared at Petra. 'Excuse me, I need to take this outside,' he said, striding through the kitchen door and into the hall, and October heard him say, 'Sorry Megan, Petra is ribbing me again.'

'Megan is his girlfriend,' Amos explained. 'They've only just got together.'

Charity giggled. 'It's so sweet, seeing the pair of them — they're like two little lovebirds.'

Nope — "lovebird" was another word October wouldn't use to describe Nathan from what she'd seen of him so far, but what did she know? She'd only met him once before. He might be a veritable Romeo, and even from that tiny glimpse of him as he answered the call, she could tell he was in love.

She didn't begrudge anyone that, despite her own recent unfortunate foray into the realms of romance. At least she hadn't had her heart broken, but she had been quite hurt though.

'Talking about being in love, how is Faith getting on in Norwich?' Petra asked Charity, and October was interested to see the differing play of emotions flitting across the girl's face at the question.

'Just so that you can keep up,' Petra said to October, 'Faith and Charity are twins. Charity's horse, Storm, is stabled here. Faith used to stable hers here too, but she moved to Norwich with her boyfriend, so she's had to sell her horse. He's still here, though. He's the big black gelding called Midnight,' she added.

'She's doing great,' Charity said. 'She's got a new job and she's sent me loads of photos of her house. They're renting at the moment, but I think they're looking for somewhere to buy.' Charity seemed a little downcast at this, but then she perked up. 'Me and Timothy are going to visit them at the end of February.'

Petra said to October, 'Timothy is Charity's boyfriend and he's a vet at the practice in Picklewick. Timothy is also Harry's brother, and Harry is my...' Petra hesitated, then followed it up with, '...partner. Not in the business sense, you understand, more in the living together sense. You'll meet him soon. He'll be back before you leave this evening. There's not an awful lot of shoeing you can do when it's dark.'

'He's a farrier?' October asked.

'That's right'.

'It must be handy having both a farrier and a vet around.'

Petra flashed her a smile. 'It certainly is! Saves me a fortune in shoeing, I can tell you. I have to pay full price for the vet service though, more's the pity.'

'How come Midnight is still here?' October asked.

Petra shrugged. 'He was bought by a guy called Luca something or other...I can never remember his name...and he asked if he could pay livery fees to stable him here. I wasn't going to say no, especially considering those fees pay some of your wages.'

'Does that mean I have to be nice to him?' October joked.

Petra snorted. 'Not if you don't want to. He comes across as a bit of a flash git, but he's okay really. He likes horses, that's the main thing.'

As far as October was concerned, that was the main thing for her, too. She could deal with flash gits – after all, her last romantic liaison had been with an incredibly flash git indeed.

Luca hadn't expected to see a strange woman in Midnight's loosebox but when he noticed how pretty she was, he didn't object. The first glimpse he had was of her behind. She was bending over, scrabbling about in the straw. It was a nice trim behind, and that alone would have been enough to concentrate his gaze, but when she straightened up and turned around, the sight of her focused his attention even more.

She was probably close to his age, maybe a year or two younger, slim but with curves where he hoped to find them, and long shapely legs encased in a pair of breeches. When his attention finally made his way to her face, it was to find her staring at him with a questioning and not particularly friendly glint in her eye.

'Can I help you?' she asked.

'Shouldn't I be asking you the same question?'

'I don't know, should you? Who are you anyway?'

'I own the horse whose box you are standing in. Who are you, and what are you doing in it?'

She blushed and bit her lip. 'Oh, sorry, I didn't realise. I work here as from today, and the reason I'm in Midnight's stall is because I've lost something.'

'Can I help you look for it?'

'No, thanks, I've looked. It's not here. I'll check the loosebox next door.'

'What exactly have you lost?'

'It's nothing. It doesn't matter.'

'Clearly it **does** matter, or you wouldn't be looking for it'.

She shrugged. 'Honestly, it's nothing; it's just a hair grip.'

He could see tendrils of her hair poking out from underneath her woolly hat. They were very dark and curled slightly around her face. Her skin was creamy and clear, and her eyes were brown, possibly with flecks of green in them. It was difficult to tell without squinting, and he thought it best not to do that – he seemed to have made her uncomfortable enough already.

'If I come across it, I'll leave it in the office,' he said. 'What does it look like?'

'It really doesn't matter.'

He waited patiently, hoping that she'd tell him in the end if he didn't say anything.

'It's a claw,' she said finally, demonstrating what she meant with her fingers and thumb. 'It's white and blue, a sort of Mediterranean design. But don't trouble yourself. I can easily get another. I took it out of my hair to put my hat on and it must have fallen out of my pocket. It's no big deal,' she insisted.

Luca couldn't help staring at her as she spoke, and he tore his gaze away from her with difficulty and glanced around the yard at the empty stalls. 'They're still out in the fields, are they?'

'If you mean the horses, then yes. If you're asking about the humans, I'm not quite sure. And the chickens could be anywhere.' Her lips twitched and her eyes twinkled.

He grinned to himself. She was sassy, and he always thought that a sense of humour in a woman was far more attractive than her looks. 'Where's the goat?' he asked.

'In the barn.'

'And Tiddles?'

'I haven't had the pleasure of meeting Tiddles, yet. I'm assuming that's a cat?'

'She certainly is. Sorry, I haven't introduced myself. I'm Luca Dalton. As I said, Midnight is my horse.' He thrust his hand through the open stable door and she stepped forward and took it awkwardly.

As they shook, he noticed how firm her grip was. He also caught a whiff of her perfume, and he slowly inhaled the gorgeous scent.

'October Rees,' she said. 'He's got good conformation and a nice neat head. What's he like to ride?'

Eh? Oh, she was talking about Midnight. 'Smooth, rocking horse canter, pacey trot. Can be a bit headstrong.'

She nodded. 'I prefer them with some spirit.'

Luca got the feeling she might be just as spirited as his horse, and a little bolt of excitement jolted him in the chest. 'Do you own your own horse?' he asked.

'Unfortunately, no.'

She looked crestfallen and Luca spoke without thinking. 'Feel free to ride Midnight whenever you like.'

Why had he done that? He didn't know a thing about her, and he certainly didn't know how well she rode. Petra and Nathan were the only people who Luca had agreed could ride his horse, although Timothy, Charity's boyfriend, had been on Midnight's back once or twice when he'd gone out with Charity for a ride. Horses were valuable creatures, especially when things went wrong, and Luca wasn't in the habit of loaning his horse to just anyone.

However, October must be a decent enough rider or Petra wouldn't have employed her. He'd read the advert she'd put out, and it did say that the successful person would be expected to teach the occasional class so October must be a competent horsewoman.

'Thanks.' October nodded and gave him a small smile which he interpreted as showing her appreciation for the offer. 'I'm sorry, you'll have to excuse me. I've still got a lot to do and I'm not quite sure where everything is yet,' she added, stepping towards the door of the loosebox.

He realised he was blocking her exit and he stood to the side to let her pass. 'I expect I'll see you around?'

'I expect so.' Her smile was polite but her eyes were friendly, and as she walked away Luca's gaze followed her.

To say he was intrigued was an understatement. To say he didn't find her attractive would be a downright lie.

He wondered whether she'd say yes if he asked her out.

Flipping heck, Petra thought. She'd never felt so shattered in all her life! Thank god she'd finally taken someone on at the stables. October Rees was overqualified for the job, but Petra wasn't complaining. Besides, she hadn't had much interest in the advert she'd put out, and she guessed the main reason might be because living accommodation wasn't included. But there was no way she wanted a stranger living under her roof, and there was nowhere else suitable.

She didn't run a big enough operation to warrant converting any of the outbuildings into flats – that sort of thing was reserved for the big racing yards and the like. Little stables such as her riding school had to rely on the local workforce, and being a stable hand (or **groom** as Megan, Nathan's girlfriend, had suggested she put in the advert) wasn't for everyone. It was hard work, the hours could be unsuitable, and you worked outside in all weathers. The wages weren't brilliant either, but Petra was offering the most she could afford and, as she'd told October during her interview, she could have all the rides she wanted. If you didn't own your own horse, that alone was worth a small fortune. Petra had also been delighted when October had told her she'd be able to teach a few lessons, freeing up Petra to do other things. Such as sleep.

Petra headed into the office, wanting to check which jobs still needed to be done for the day and which could be put off until tomorrow, when she ran straight into the woman she'd just been thinking about.

'Oops, sorry,' October cried, reaching out to steady her.

'My fault,' Petra said. 'I wasn't looking where I was going.' She'd been too busy yawning. 'How did your first day go?' she asked, moving around to stand in front of the whiteboard and scanning it quickly.

'It's good; nothing I haven't done before.'

'Are you enjoying it so far?'

'Yes, I am.'

'It must be a far cry from what you've been used to.'

'I suppose it is…'

Petra hadn't delved too deeply into why October had left a prestigious showjumping yard to work in a small stable in Picklewick. Of course she'd checked October's references, and she had been given a glowing one by her previous employer, but when she'd asked why October had left, she had been informed it was due to personal reasons. The man she'd spoken to had been at pains to clarify that those personal reasons weren't a reflection on October's suitability for employment.

As soon as she'd met October, Petra had felt an affinity to her. They were around the same age and they both loved working with horses, although that was where the similarities ended. Their paths had been very different. Petra, although she didn't technically own the stables, knew that if anything happened to Amos she would inherit it. Also, she had carte blanche on how the riding school was run. Amos rarely interfered anymore. Although **he** wouldn't call it interfering, he'd call it "guiding" or "helping out".

October, on the other hand, had worked for some very famous people in the showjumping world. And, although Petra wasn't certain, she'd sensed that October had wanted a slice of that particular pie for herself; but maybe she wasn't talented enough, or maybe she simply hadn't been able to afford it, or she hadn't had the right breaks or the right kind of luck. Petra didn't know. All that mattered was that October was a good rider, a good worker, and cared about horses as much as Petra herself did.

However, she had a feeling October would move on at some point, although Petra hoped she would stick around for a while. It was the only reservation Petra had had when she'd offered October the job. Petra would hate to get used to October, only for her to leave after a couple of months, but she hadn't had a great deal of choice because she'd not had any other applicants.

October said, 'I'm just going to bring the horses in and get them settled, and then I'm done for the day. Is that okay?'

Petra yawned again. 'Sorry, I've been overdoing it. We've been shorthanded for a while. See you tomorrow.'

'Bye,' October replied, and Petra watched her leave.

As soon as she was alone Petra slumped onto the desk, resting her backside on the edge of it, feeling washed out. She'd been feeling like this for a while, and she was fairly certain she'd been fighting off a bug. However, this bug had been hanging around for six to eight weeks and it didn't seem to be going anywhere. She wished it would develop into something proper, so she could get it over and done with. Feeling crap for nearly two months wasn't fun.

Occasionally she caught Harry, Amos or Nathan giving her sideways glances, and she knew they were all concerned about her, but she told them the same thing she'd been telling herself – that she'd had much more work to do since Faith had stopped coming to the stables to help out, and then there had been Christmas and all the fuss leading up to it, so it was no wonder she'd hardly had a minute to draw breath. Plus the winter months were always difficult financially for the stables, so she was also worried about paying the bills. Hopefully, now that October was here and spring was on the horizon, she was bound to feel more like her normal lively self soon.

Wasn't she?

'Is everything okay?' Petra asked. She was snuggled under the duvet with only the top of her head and her nose poking out and Harry thought she looked incredibly cute, if somewhat tired. When he first met her, no way on earth would he have described her as cute – prickly, argumentative, stubborn, defensive, but never cute. She was still all of those things, but he could see the kind, loving, loyal and incredibly beautiful soul beneath. And when she was peering out of the bedclothes at him with her hair all messed up, he thought she was the most gorgeous woman in the world. And she was **his.**

He shrugged off his dressing gown and slipped in naked beside her, still damp from the shower he'd had after doing his usual check around the stables before bedtime.

'It's fine,' he said. 'Everything is locked up and everyone is sleeping. Apart from Fred. I could hear that darned cockerel chundering away to himself in the coop. The hens won't be happy if he keeps them awake all night.'

'Neither will I, because a grumpy hen won't lay.'

Harry turned onto his side and propped himself up on his elbow. 'How was October's first day?'

'Good, I think.'

'Let's hope she'll take some of the strain off you.'

'Let's hope she'll stay around long enough,' Petra retorted.

'Why wouldn't she?' Harry was puzzled.

'There's not enough to keep her here horse-wise, plus the wages aren't great. As you know the problem is that the big racing and showjumping yards have live-in grooms. Having your accommodation provided is quite a perk.'

Harry kissed her on the nose. 'It can't be helped. You can't afford to pay her more.'

'At least she's living with her mum, so she doesn't have a mortgage or rent to pay, although she told me that she's helping with the bills,' Petra said.

'Do you think she'd stay if we had suitable accommodation?' he asked slowly, an idea beginning to form.

'Maybe. I don't know.' She yawned hugely, then gave him a plaintive look.

'I'm starving,' she said, sleepily, 'but I can't be bothered to get anything to eat.'

Harry grinned, guessing she was hoping he'd offer to nip down to the kitchen and fetch her something. 'I'll make you a snack. What would you like? Toast? Omelette? Sandwich?'

'Peanut butter.'

'You hate peanut butter.'

'I don't.'

'You do,' he insisted. He loved it but she'd never been able to stomach the stuff (her words). He felt the same way about Marmite, but she adored it.

'I've changed my mind – I fancy some.'

Harry smiled down at her fondly. 'Okay, peanut butter it is. On toast?

'No, with bananas. And some yoghurt.'

'Really?'

She nodded.

He reached across to give her a squeeze but as he did so she winced. 'What's wrong?'

'My damned bra shrank in the wash and it's been cutting into me all day, so now I'm a bit sore. A few other things have shrunk too. I'll have to have a word with Amos. He still can't get to grips with the new washing machine and we've had it a couple of months now. I'll have no clothes left at this rate.'

Harry got out of bed and put his dressing gown back on. 'I can't say I've noticed any problem with my clothes.'

Petra glared at him. She reminded him of Princess when she was cross. That goat had a mean look in her eye when she was upset. 'So it's just my stuff he's shrinking, is it? Great!'

Chuckling to himself, Harry made his way downstairs. Peanut butter indeed! It was rather nice with bananas, but he hadn't tried it with a scoop of yoghurt dolloped over the top.

After he'd made Petra her snack, he had a quick taste. Mmm, not bad. He must remember to have this for breakfast tomorrow. Healthy and nutritious, and very tasty. Nice one, Petra, he thought, as he carried the bowl and a spoon back to their bedroom.

Closing the door quietly behind him, he began, 'It's quite nice—' Then he stopped.

Petra was fast asleep, bless her.

Harry used his free hand to stroke a strand of hair off her face, love filling him so completely that he thought he might explode from the force of it. He never thought he'd feel this way about anyone.

Smiling ruefully, he put the bowl and spoon to one side in case she woke and was still hungry, then he eased himself into bed, careful not to disturb her. With a contented sigh, he turned onto his side and spooned her, wrapping his arms around her waist and gently pulling her close, then he winced when she half woke up and pushed at him.

'Sore,' she muttered, and he realised he was crushing her to him rather too tightly.

'Sorry,' he murmured, loosening his grip, and was relieved when she immediately sank back into slumber. She looked as though she needed all the sleep she could get.

He hoped she would slow down and be able to take a step back now that she had October to help her. He desperately wanted for them to be able to spend more time together, just the two of them, which wasn't easy when she was running such a time-consuming business as the stables.

Harry wanted nothing more than to spend every moment with this wonderful woman and as he lay there in the cocooned darkness, listening to her soft breathing, he thought how lucky he was to have found her.

CHAPTER TWO

A couple of days later, Luca was leaning against the railings surrounding the gallery, his eyes trained on the woman in the centre of the arena who was teaching a small class of novice riders. Petra was by his side, and she was equally as focused.

'What do you think?' he asked quietly out of the side of his mouth, without taking his eyes off October.

'She certainly knows what she's doing,' Petra said. 'Not that it's any of your business.'

'I was just asking,' Luca replied, feeling slightly hurt. Petra could often be prickly, but she was definitely grouchier lately.

She must have realised how grumpy she sounded because she turned to him and said, 'Sorry, I'm a bit short tempered. Not enough sleep and too much to do. I'm quite impressed with her: she's patient, kind, and calm, and she's got a nice way about her. She'll do.'

Luca was pleased about that. He'd only just met October, and he'd hate for her to be sent away with a flea in her ear. There was no fear of that though, because Luca could also see how good she was. She'd be an asset to the stables and no mistake.

He wondered where she was from. He didn't live in Picklewick himself; he lived just outside, but he hadn't been there all that long, having only bought his house in the summer, and he wasn't fully integrated into village life yet, and hadn't got to know many people so far.

Luca glanced at his watch and was pleased to see there was only another ten minutes of the lesson to go; he couldn't wait to put Midnight through his paces.

He'd done a little bit of jumping with him, but not much, so he was looking forward to getting on the horse and seeing what he could do. He'd already checked with Petra to make sure the arena wouldn't be needed after this lesson, and as long as he put the jumps away and tidied up after himself, she had been more than happy to let him loose in there.

He watched for another few minutes as October gave each young rider another turn over the low jumps then, when she called the lesson to a halt, he left the gallery and went back out into the yard to fetch Midnight. Luca had already saddled him, so it didn't take him long before he was back in the arena, the horse in tow.

'Hi,' he said, nodding and smiling to Charity who had come in to loosen girths and slide the stirrup irons up their leather straps ready to take the ponies back to their respective stalls.

She stopped for a moment to make a fuss of the horse that used to belong to her sister, and the gelding snickered a greeting and nuzzled his nose into her, probably looking for a mint or a horse nut.

Charity duly produced a mint from her pocket and held it out, and Midnight snaffled it up with his mobile whiskery lips and crunched contentedly. Most ponies and horses loved mints, and it was a nice little treat for them without having to worry about additional calories. Luca always had a packet about his person, too.

'There's no need to bother,' he called out suddenly, seeing October starting to put

away the jumps. 'I'll be using those,' he
added.

Luca tied Midnight to a tethering ring set
into the wall and strolled across the arena
floor, his boots sinking into the sand, and
debated what height he should place the
poles at. He decided he'd start the horse
off fairly low to warm him up, then he'd
give him a bit of a stretch and a
challenge.

It took Luca a few minutes to arrange the
jumps to his satisfaction and to make
sure they were at the correct height, and
by that time Charity and October had
taken the ponies out and he was on his
own.

Swinging himself into the saddle, Luca
took his mount on a couple of laps around
the arena first, to make sure the horse
was paying attention and listening to him
when he asked him to trot or canter, and
when he was satisfied that Midnight was
behaving himself, Luca did one final

circuit and then aimed him at the nearest jump.

Cantering slowly up to it, the horse popped over the fence with the minimum of effort, and he did the same with the next three. Happy with the way things were going, Luca dismounted and raised the height on the bars, before moving one of the jumps to allow for the horse's increased stride.

Satisfied, Luca mounted up again, and took him over the new height.

It was as he was approaching the last one that a movement out of the corner of his eye caught Luca's attention, and he glanced up to see October lurking at the back of the gallery, as though she didn't want to be seen.

Luca pretended he hadn't noticed her and he carried on about his business, once more getting off Midnight, raising the bars another notch, and mounting up again.

He'd gone a little higher than he'd intended, and he knew he was in danger of showing off. He wasn't normally like that but he found himself wanting to impress her, and Luca got the feeling that his ability to handle a horse would be more important to the new stable hand than what car he drove or what job he did. He wanted her to think well of him and his ability to handle Midnight.

Luca wasn't a novice jumper and neither was he new to horse ownership. He'd been around horses all his life, having ridden since he was five, but he'd never been seriously competitive and he therefore hadn't joined the Pony Club or competed in any major gymkhanas. He had only wanted to ride for pleasure, but he did get a buzz and an adrenaline rush when he rode over jumps.

He knew he was lucky to be able to afford to own a horse. They weren't cheap to buy, but that wasn't the issue; the problem was their upkeep. A set of shoes roughly every six weeks, plus all the feed, plus the vet bills, plus the insurance – it soon added up. Not to mention having to find grazing, and pay livery fees. It was unfortunate that he wasn't able to see to his horse himself every day, but his job had to take precedence and at least he knew Midnight was well looked after at the stables on Muddypuddle Lane. Petra ran a tight ship, and Luca was more than happy with the care she provided for his mount.

Right, he thought, **let's have a go at this, my boy, and see what you can do**. He hadn't tried the horse over jumps this high before, and he supposed he should put them down a couple of notches. But they were there now, and as he took Midnight for a lap around the arena before he tackled the first fence, Luca risked a very swift glance at the gallery.

October was barely visible in the gloom, but he knew she was watching him.

Midnight pricked his ears as he straightened up to face the first jump, and Luca aimed him at it. The horse knew perfectly well what was expected, and Luca reined him in slightly to allow him to gather his hindquarters under him. Before he gave Midnight his head, he felt the animal's power and knew the horse would have no trouble clearing this height.

The constrained canter lasted for a few paces, then Luca leaned over the horse's neck to give him more rein and braced himself for the jump.

Midnight landed perfectly, and no sooner had he done so than Luca gathered him up again and pointed him at the next hurdle.

Yes! he thought silently as Midnight took this one in his stride too, and Luca turned him into the last jump, going wide to make sure the horse had enough time to both see it and to prepare for it.

That was the point where things started to go wrong.

Midnight, for some inexplicable reason of his own, took an instant dislike to the fence he'd already jumped twice before, albeit at a slightly lower elevation, and just as Luca thought the animal was about to take it, the horse changed his mind and juddered to a halt.

Luca went sailing over the horse's ears and fell unceremoniously on the other side of the fence in a winded heap.

'Oof!' Not the most dignified of sounds.

He sat up slowly, rubbing his shoulder.

Thankfully, nothing was broken, and he didn't appear to be hurt apart from his pride. *That'll teach me to show off,* he thought ruefully.

Feeling a bit of an idiot, he clambered to his feet, dusted himself down, and went to catch his horse.

Midnight, though, had other ideas. The animal was quite happy to not have a rider on his back and was trotting around the arena with his head and his tail held high, his ears pricked forward and a smug, self-satisfied look on his face. If horses could snigger, Midnight would be laughing his horseshoes off.

It was as Luca was debating whether to run around after the horse or wait for Midnight to get fed up and come to him, that he realised he was no longer alone; October had slipped silently into the arena and was standing just behind him.

'Do you need a hand?' she asked, and he could hear the amusement in her voice.

'No thanks, I can manage.'

'It looks like it.'

'He'll get fed up before I will.

'I don't think so. If you go that way and I go this, we can trap him in a corner.' October was grinning broadly.

'I swear to god he knows what he's doing,' Luca groaned.

'Of course he does. He's having great fun.'

'And you aren't?' Luca asked her, with a raised eyebrow.

'I suppose I am.' She sent him a wicked smile.

Luca caught his breath. The bolt of desire that shot through him was a surprise. He thought she was pretty, beautiful even, and he was seriously attracted to her, but the reaction he'd just had was visceral, felt deep in his gut, and it floored him.

He cleared his throat to cover his confusion and started walking towards Midnight, who was at the far end of the arena. The horse had come to a halt, but he continued to be on full alert, staring at them with his ears pricked forward, daring Luca to come any closer.

The horse let him get within about three metres, then he jerked his head up, whirled on his haunches and trotted off. Luca was positive the animal was looking over his shoulder and laughing at him.

October hadn't moved. She was watching intently, a smile playing about her lips. Then she calmly stuck her hand in a pocket and pulled out a carrot.

'That's cheating!' Luca exclaimed.

'All's fair in love and catching horses,' October retorted. She whistled, attracting the horse's attention.

Midnight, still circling at the far end, turned to look at her, his ears flicking back and forth.

'Look what I've got,' she said to him.

The horse looked, and he mut have liked what he saw because he trotted a few paces, then stopped a short distance away and huffed.

'You're going to have to come a little closer if you want your carrot,' October told him.

Luca could see the exact moment the horse admitted defeat and decided the carrot was worth more than his short burst of freedom. He seemed to slump slightly as if he'd had his fun and he now wanted to eat his treat and return to his stable.

Luca didn't blame him; after the fiasco of falling off with October witnessing his ignominy, he felt much the same way himself.

As the horse walked up to her, Midnight stretched out his neck, delicately took the carrot between his mobile hairy lips and began to crunch on it. October reached around and grabbed hold of his bridle.

Midnight gave Luca a sideways look and Luca narrowed his eyes at him. The horse may have won this round, but there would be plenty of others.

'I'll take him back to his stall if you want,' October said, but Luca shook his head.

'It's okay, I'll see to him. He's my horse and you've probably got enough to do.' He was wishing she'd go away so he could nurse his wounded pride in peace.

'I don't mind giving you a hand.' She lifted Midnight's reins over his head to

use them to lead him with and gave them
to Luca. 'He was going so well, too,'
October said, and he heard a hint of
laughter in her voice.

'Do you jump much?' he asked,
innocently.

'Some.'

Luca made no move to leave the arena.
Instead, he turned to her and said, 'Do
you fancy having a go?'

'Me ride Midnight?'

He smiled. 'Of course, you don't have to if
you're worried you might come off.'

'Like you did, you mean?'

Luca shrugged, admitting the truth of it.
But he'd attempted a decent height, and
he didn't believe she would do any better.

'Go on, then.' She held out her hand for the reins and he gave them back to her and stood aside.

'Do you need a leg-up getting on him?' he asked, but even before he'd finished the sentence October was on the horse's back and staring down at him.

'I think I can manage,' she said.

Luca shook his head. That showed him. 'Should I hang around here in case you...?' He trailed off, gesturing towards the jumps and wondering how soon she'd come a cropper. Midnight, Luca had discovered, could be a handful.

'Fall off?' She turned the horse's head and urged him into a trot, shouting back over her shoulder, 'Nah, you're okay. Sit in the gallery and get yourself a coffee.'

Smiling to himself, Luca was impressed with her spirit. If that was the way she wanted to play it...

October took Midnight for a canter around the arena. He was biddable enough now that he'd got his rebellion out of his system, but she could also sense the horse would be quick to take advantage of any sign of weakness on her part.

'Oh, no, you don't, my laddo,' she murmured to him when he tossed his head, not liking the short rein she was keeping him on.

He crabbed sideways and tossed his head again, but when he realised he wasn't going to get his own way and that the rider on his back was in charge and not him, Midnight settled down and behaved himself.

For the moment.

October wasn't fooled. She'd met his sort on more than one occasion and she knew precisely how to deal with him. You had to show him who was boss and take charge from the beginning, or he'd walk all over you.

As she took Midnight around for a second time to make sure he was settled and focused, a thought occurred to her. She **was** referring to the horse, wasn't she? Not the man who owned it?

If the cap fits...

Not that she intended to have any more of a relationship with Luca than she had with his horse. Caring for Midnight was part and parcel of her new job. His owner was, to a certain extent irrelevant, as far as October was concerned.

He was damnably good-looking though, she was forced to admit, as she caught a glimpse of him out of the corner of her eye.

He was in the gallery, leaning nonchalantly against the wall, a cup of something hot in his hand and a smug expression on his face, and she realised that he was expecting her to come off.

Ha! Not a chance. She'd been watching Midnight carefully whilst Luca had been in the arena with him, and she knew precisely the point at which the horse was would be tempted to baulk at the jump. All she needed was to urge him on just as he considered refusing to jump it, and the wind would be taken out of the animal's sails. He'd pop over the fence without a second thought.

Anyway, it wasn't particularly high, and October knew she could get more out of this horse with a bit of encouragement. It would do for now though, to prove a point.

Luca was an arrogant so-and-so and a bit patronising, and she'd love nothing better than to see the smug expression wiped off his face when he realised she wasn't going to be thrown off.

Sitting upright and slightly back in the saddle, she lined Midnight up for the first jump, holding him back with practised ease, relishing the control she had over him. It was exhilarating to think she had half a tonne of horse underneath her, behaving itself impeccably, and she could tell that Midnight was keen by the way he held his head and the bunching power of his hindquarters. His ears were pointing towards the jump, and October stared through them and beyond, still holding him back.

Then abruptly she released him and he exploded towards the fence, tucked his front hooves neatly underneath his chest and popped over the jump with minimum effort and absolutely no fuss whatsoever.

Then she asked him to do the same a further four times until he'd cleared all the jumps, joy bubbling through her. God, she'd missed this!

Careful to keep her expression neutral (she didn't want Luca to think she was gloating, even though she secretly was), she brought Midnight to a standstill and slid gracefully off his back.

A slow clap echoed around the arena.

October ignored it.

She didn't acknowledge Luca until he was standing right next to her, and even then she didn't dare look him in the eye. Instead, she busied herself by sorting out the horse's stirrups and loosening his girth.

'That was...' Luca paused. 'Clean.'

'Clean is good,' she replied, accepting the compliment. She could guess how she and the horse had looked – controlled, graceful, effortless, neat, popping over the jumps with ease.

When she finally met Luca's eye, she was intrigued by what she saw. Respect – she'd been hoping to see that. But there was also desire smouldering in their depths, which drew an answering response from her as butterflies fluttered into life in her stomach.

After what had happened at her last stables, she didn't think she'd feel anything but a low-key despair when it came to men, but she surprised herself. **Luca** surprised her.

'Good jumping,' he said. 'I'm impressed. You must think me a right jerk after my little stunt.'

She gave him a wry smile. 'Perhaps.'

'I should have known better.'

'Agreed.' She handed him Midnight's reins. 'I take it you're going to bed him down?'

His eyes widened and she could simply tell that he was imaging taking **her** to bed. In your dreams, she felt like saying, so it wasn't unexpected when he asked, 'Will you have dinner with me tonight?'

What she hadn't anticipated was her reply. 'I'd like that.'

And she would – she most definitely would.

'I've been thinking,' Harry said, walking into their bedroom, wrapping his arms around Petra and cuddling into her. He hoped his idea might be the solution to the stables' financial problems, but initially it was going to take money, time and hard work before Petra and Amos would start to reap the benefits. Hard work wasn't an issue – none of them was averse to that; however, time might be a problem because he didn't know how long his idea would take to implement, or how long the stables could keep going without an upturn in their finances; which brought him to the main stumbling block – money.

Petra groaned. 'What about? It had better not be silly.' She had been changing out of her work clothes and into jogging bottoms and a fleece, and Harry saw her give her jodhpurs a grim look. Oh dear, he thought, Amos must still be having trouble with the programmes on the washing machine.

'It isn't silly,' Harry protested, then added. 'Okay, you might think it is, but hear me out before you say anything?'

'Go on...'

'How about we convert the cowshed into living accommodation?'

'For October?'

'For paying guests. Although it might also help to persuade October to stay at the stables if we could throw in somewhere to live.'

'I suspect a certain horse owner might help her do that just as successfully, and without us having to go to all the expense of building a house for her.'

Harry was derailed for a moment. 'What do you mean?'

'She fancies Luca and he fancies her. You ought to have seen them this afternoon. They were in the arena together and they couldn't take their eyes off one another.'

'Interesting... But I didn't mean somewhere for October to live – I was thinking about holiday rentals. We're not using the cowshed for anything.'

Petra slid out of his arms and sat on the edge of the bed to wiggle a clean pair of socks over her toes. 'Do you think my ankles look puffy?'

Harry bent down for a better look. 'Not that I can see. They look the same as usual.'

'Hmm.' She frowned as she rotated her foot, turning her leg this way and that. 'It's being used for storage,' she said.

Harry pulled a face. 'I've seen what's in there.' Some of the stuff had been "stored" since the last World War.

She shrugged. 'It might come in useful one day.'

'When?'

'I don't know, do I?'

'When was the last time you made use of anything in there?'

'Um...?'

'Exactly!'

'It's a great idea, but it's not feasible. What about the expense for a start, and who's going to run it? I've got too much to do as it is.'

'I'm not suggesting turning it into a five-star luxury hotel. I reckon we could get three two-bed holiday lets out of it. It'll take a bit of work but once they're up and running they'll bring more money in for minimum effort than anything else in the stables.'

'What about the initial outlay? It's going to cost a fortune to do the renovations.'

'There is that—' he began, but Petra waved a hand at him, yawning.

'Can we talk about it another time? I'm too tired to discuss it now,' she said.

She did look exhausted. He'd been hoping that now she had October working for her, she would be able to slow down and take some time off. But if anything, she looked even more tired.

'Of course. It was only a thought...' he said. 'Let's see what Amos has made for dinner, then you can veg out in front of the TV.'

He waited for her to finish putting her socks on and held the door open.

As she went to walk through it, she stopped and reached up to stroke his face. 'I really appreciate you trying to help,' she said. 'Have I told you I love you?'

'Not for at least an hour,' he said, pressing his face into the palm of her hand. 'I love you too.'

Her smile took his breath away. 'I know,' she whispered, and his heart flooded with joy.

Luca was unaccountably nervous. This was a meal in a gastropub. Nothing more. He'd taken many a woman on dates in similar places. What was there to be nervous about?

Possibly because none of them had made his heart race the way October did?

Telling himself not to be ridiculous, he pulled up outside the address she'd given him and debated whether to beep the horn, ring the doorbell, or text her to say he was at the kerb.

Whilst he sat there dithering, her front door opened and he stared at the figure illuminated by the hall light. He caught a brief glimpse of her, before she pulled the door closed and was dashing down the path.

He leaned across the passenger seat, cranked the door handle and October got in.

'Nice car,' she said. 'Is it new?'

'I've had it a while.' He smiled at her, using the excuse of checking that she'd put her seatbelt on to give her a closer look.

What he saw made his mouth go dry.

She looked stunning. Her hair was loose and she'd curled it at the ends, she'd put smoky stuff around her eyes, her lashes looked longer and fuller than he remembered, and her lips were tinted red. Not only that, the boots had three-inch heels and her legs were endless, encased as they were in black tights. She was wearing a short skirt, which she tucked around her thighs as she settled herself in the passenger seat, and a knitted top with a coat over it.

He swallowed hard.

'You've got **two** cars?' she asked.

'Um, yeah? Is that a problem?'

'Not at all. Although you've got to admit, it is a bit greedy.' She grinned at him, and he decided she must be pulling his leg. 'What make is it?' she asked.

'An Aston Martin. It's quite an old one,' he added, as if to justify the expense. He was about to tell her that cars were his one weakness but he'd be lying. He had many weaknesses, and they were all for the finer things in life. Luca usually made no apology for that – he'd worked hard to get where he was – but somehow this woman made him feel tacky about it.

'It's gorgeous,' she said. 'Not very practical though.'

'Which is why I also drive a Range Rover.'

'I've got a Ford.'

'I know, I've seen it in the car park.'

Silence followed, and Luca concentrated on his driving as they seemed to have exhausted that particular topic of conversation.

'What do you do for a living?' she asked eventually, and he wondered if she was feeling as awkward as he.

Maybe asking her out wasn't such a good idea if the only thing they had in common was horses. 'I own a tech company.'

'Do you want to expand on that?'

'It's not very exciting,' he said. At least, not for other people, although he tended to find it fascinating.

'Try me,' she said, and he heard the challenge in her voice.

'Okay, you asked for it,' he replied, and for the next twenty minutes he regaled her with details about how he first started up, what his business was all about now, and where he saw it going in the future. 'What about you?' he asked, when he guessed he must have bored her enough. To be fair to her, she'd asked loads of questions and had seemed genuinely interested.

'I'm a stable hand,' she said. 'You know that.'

'I suspect there's more to you than that,' he retorted. 'Such as, where did you work before?'

'A showjumping yard in Kent.'

'What brought you to Picklewick?'

'My mother moved here a few years ago and now that my granny has gone into a care home, she's lonely. So I thought I'd move back in and keep her company.'

He gave her a sceptical look – there was something in her tone which made him think she wasn't telling him the whole story. But even if that were the case, it was none of his business.

Changing the subject he said, 'You're a fab rider.'

'Thanks. You're not too bad yourself.'

'You're humouring me.'

'I'm telling the truth. It helps if you can stay on, though.'

'Ha, ha.' Luca indicated left and drove into the gastro pub's car park. 'Here we are.'

When they walked inside, Luca having sped around to October's side of the car to give her a hand getting out (the sports car was rather low-slung for elegant exits), he noticed her quick scrutiny of the place.

'Is it okay?' he asked, concerned that maybe he should have taken her somewhere flashier.

'It's nice,' she said, and once they had been shown to a table and were seated, she added, 'When I saw the car, I thought we might be going somewhere really expensive.'

Luca frowned. 'Would that have been a problem?'

'Yes. I intend we go Dutch.'

'I asked you out, so I'm paying.'

'No. You are not. Dutch,' she insisted.

He sighed. 'As you wish.' He'd been about to order a nice bottle of wine, but he thought better of it, and when she asked for water with a twist of lime, he also understood she was being sensible – he'd forgotten that she probably had to be at the stables early in the morning.

So far, this evening wasn't going quite as he'd expected, but then nothing about October was as expected. For one thing, she wasn't particularly forthcoming about herself and it intrigued him.

He had a feeling he was going to enjoy getting to know her better.

Luca might come across as a bit of a show-off, but October had a feeling it wasn't his true self, she thought as she studied him over dinner. Like the way he'd seemed nervous when he asked if the pub was okay. He'd appeared uncertain, as though he might be worried that he'd brought her to the wrong place. It was quite endearing.

He'd also been rather self-deprecating when he was telling her about his business. She guessed it had probably taken a great deal of determination and drive to build it from such humble beginnings, not to mention a considerable degree of business acumen, skill and creativity. He'd skimmed over all those things when she'd mentioned them, and he'd put it down to luck.

Or was it merely an act to get into her knickers? The problem was that she was used to Zeus's false modesty and he'd used it most effectively to get her to sleep with him, that it had made her wary.

Slowly October and Luca discovered more about each other, superficial things mostly such as what kind of music they liked, what bands they'd seen, the films they'd watched, and of course, horsey stuff. She lived and breathed horses, and at least he enjoyed riding and he seemed to enjoy hearing about her adventures in the showjumping world. She hadn't always worked for Zeus Fernsby (she resisted the childish urge to cross herself to ward off his particular brand of awfulness), and she had many tales of behind-the-scenes disasters and near misses.

In turn, Luca told her stories about some of his more difficult and demanding clients, and how some of them expected him to be on call to answer their questions or solve a problem at all hours of the day and even in the middle of the night.

Both October and Luca were discreet enough not to mention any names, and she was glad of this because she preferred not to go into detail about her time working for Zeus. The less said about that the better.

Eventually, though, they'd outstayed their welcome in the pub (the staff were dropping them big hints by cleaning up around them) and after a brief tussle over the bill (she won the argument and insisted on paying half) they found themselves in the car heading towards Picklewick.

'I've had a good time tonight,' Luca said, keeping his eyes on the road.

'Don't sound so surprised,' she shot back.

'I'm not,' he protested, then saw her grin and realised she was teasing him.

Taking pity on him, she said, 'I did, too.'

'I'm paying next time.'

'Who says there will be a next time?' She raised an eyebrow.

'Oh, but I thought—'

'Kidding.' Her voice softened as she added, 'I'd like that.'

'Me paying?'

'There being a next time. I was hoping there would be – but we're still going Dutch.'

'You're a very stubborn woman, October Rees.' He drew the car to a halt outside her house, leaving the engine running.

'Yeah, but you like it,' she retorted.

'I like **you**. What are you doing on Saturday?'

'Nothing.'

'You are now – if you want,' he added, and she heard the tone of his voice change from confident to uncertain.

'I want,' she told him.

'Good...'

She saw him hesitate as she reached for the door handle, and she wondered if he was going to kiss her, so she tilted her face, offering her cheek.

But at the last moment she changed her mind and turned her head, and his mouth met hers and suddenly they were kissing. Nothing heavy, just his lips fluttering against hers, teasing, tantalising, promising much more...

To say she was tempted was an understatement, especially when her pulse soared and a bolt of desire shot through her, but she pulled away, slightly breathless from the force of her reaction, and left it at that.

She'd not long come out of a relationship (such as it was – the relationship being all in her deluded mind, because for Zeus it had been more of an employee with benefits kind of thing) and she had no intention of rushing into a new one, no matter how much she was attracted to

Luca. Or how much she enjoyed his company.

But even as she got out of the car and waved goodbye, she was already looking forward to seeing him again. She was looking forward to it a lot.

CHAPTER THREE

Although Petra was convinced that Harry's idea was a pie-in-the-sky one, it was now firmly lodged in her head and she'd been thinking about it all yesterday evening and today, too. If it wasn't for the immense financial outlay to get the conversion done, it could be the answer to the stables' money problems.

The finances weren't in dire straits, but neither were they blooming and it was a constant and daily battle to keep the bank balance in the black. To have a source of income that didn't involve a great deal of daily input from her once it was up and running, would also be very welcome. She'd have to consider change-over days and whether any interim attention (such as bed-making or bathroom cleaning) would be needed during the lets, or whether she could leave the holidaymakers to get on with it, but she could probably come to some arrangement with one of the villagers if necessary.

But she was getting ahead of herself.

The first thing she had to do was to find out how much it would cost. She suspected they'd need an architect, and they'd definitely need planning permission. But after that, a lot would depend on how much work they would be able to do themselves and how much a builder would charge. She'd seen enough property renovation programmes to know that any kind of build always went over budget and over time.

Nathan might be a good person to speak to. He had a decent head on his shoulders and wouldn't pussyfoot around. If he thought it was a daft idea, he'd tell her.

Of course, if she was serious about this, she also needed to speak to Amos at some point. He owned the stables, and the building works would involve some considerable up-front costs – although, at the moment, she had no idea where the money was going to come from, but until she could think of a plan to finance the work there was little point in discussing it with him.

Her thoughts whirling, Petra went in search of Nathan; she wanted to sound him out while the idea was still fresh in her head and before she'd had a chance to talk herself out of it.

Nathan was in the barn when she caught up with him, and she automatically checked the amount of hay and silage, to gauge whether there was enough feed to see them through the next month, or whether she needed to order any in.

'Can I pick your brains?' she asked, satisfied for the moment that she didn't need to place any orders.

'For what it's worth,' Nathan said, stretching to ease the kinks out of his back. He'd been pouring over the baler, and he had grease and oil on his hands.

'Have you fixed it yet?' she asked, hoping that he had. The baler was an essential piece of kit if they were to harvest their own hay.

'Nearly. What's up?'

Petra wrinkled her nose. 'Harry has this idea of transforming the cowshed into holiday lets. What do you think?'

She braced herself for a negative reaction but was surprised when he said, 'I think it's a grand idea.'

She pulled a face. 'I don't know if we can afford it.'

'How much will it cost, if you don't mind me asking?'

'I don't know.'

'Before you go any further, wouldn't it be a good idea to get a ballpark figure?'

He was right. She honestly didn't have a clue how much something like this would cost. Or how she'd manage to fit in supervising building works as well as everything else.

'I think we'd have to get an architect first,' she said. 'Harry thought the shed could be made into three cottages. What do you think?'

'Shall we take a wander over there?' Nathan suggested. His eyes were shining, and he looked quite enthused.

'I suppose.' Petra was both excited and terrified at the same time. It would be a fantastic thing to do and a great boost to the riding school's income once it was completed, but the thought of spending all that money made her feel quite ill. Perhaps they could do some of the work themselves?

It was an option to be considered, but she was exhausted just thinking about it, and she wondered how much longer it was going to take before she felt the benefit of having October around to help – because she was getting more and more knackered by the day.

Luca leaned back in his plush office chair and stretched out his legs, putting his hands behind his head. He should be concentrating on the needs of one of his most prestigious clients, but October was in his thoughts and he couldn't seem to dislodge her.

She wasn't anything like the women he normally dated. He couldn't remember the last time anyone had insisted they pay half the bill when he took them out. What usually happened was that his date ordered the most expensive thing on the menu and was more than happy to drink bottles of wine costing an arm and a leg.

October had drunk **water**, for goodness' sake. And she'd not picked at her food and wasted half of it – she'd eaten more than he had. And neither had she felt it necessary to explain why she was hungry, which one of his dates had once done. October had eaten heartily, had asked for the dessert menu, and had also enjoyed a full-fat cappuccino afterwards.

It made a refreshing change.

She'd also been funny and witty, and had displayed a keen intelligence. When he'd gently teased her, she'd given as good as she'd got. Better, in fact.

He'd thoroughly enjoyed the evening – especially the last part, where he'd kissed her.

He hadn't been sure she was going to let him, so he'd originally gone in for a peck on the cheek, but their lips had met and...Wow. Just wow.

He'd never felt so turned on by a simple kiss. There hadn't been any tongues or petting – just a gentle, tentative touch. But it had sent all his senses spiralling. And now she was stuck in his head and refusing to leave.

Luca smiled. He quite liked having her there, and he reached for his phone.

'What are you doing tonight?' he asked as soon as she answered.

'We've got a date on Saturday, remember? Or can't you wait?' Her voice was teasing and it sent a delicious shiver through him.

He didn't want to wait until Saturday. He wanted to see her now. This evening.

'What are you doing tonight?' he repeated.

'Nothing.'

Once again, that was unexpected; other women might have played hard to get.

'Do you fancy going ice skating?' For some reason, he didn't want to wine and dine her in a stuffy restaurant or a too-posh wine bar. He wanted to do something **fun**.

There was a pause. 'Where's the nearest rink?'

'Not sure. I believe there's one in the West Midlands.'

'It's a fair distance.'

'Do you mind? I'll throw in dinner,' he added, to sweeten the deal.

'You'd better had. After all that exercise, I expect to be fed. But it'll have to wait until Saturday. Some of us have to work.'

'What time do you finish?'

'Four.'

'Hang on.' Luca hurried over to his desk and clicked on a search engine. 'Are you still there?' he asked after a few seconds.

'I'm here.'

'It's open until eight o'clock this evening. I've just booked online. Pick you up at four-thirty? Or do you need more time to get ready?'

'Huh! Four-thirty is fine.'

'You might want to bring a change of clothes,' he advised.

'Oh? Why?'

'Because you'll have a wet backside from falling on it so often.'

'Hah! You wish. Whoever falls over the most gets to buy dinner. And it won't be me, sunshine.'

'Challenge accepted.' Luca was left with a huge grin on his face and excitement in his belly.

October stared at her phone incredulously then she glanced out of the window, wondering whether she'd imagined the message on it. The view from the tack room was dreary; lowering clouds, heavy with rain, the smudged grey of distant hills, and the lights already glowing from the farmhouse even though it was only two-thirty in the afternoon. Typical mid-winter gloom.

She looked back at her phone.

Nope, she hadn't imagined it. Zeus and Minnow had broken up. Again.

And Zeus thought she should hear it from him before she heard it from anyone else. Which was thoughtful of him. It was a pity he hadn't been as thoughtful in letting her know that he and his wife had got back together in the first place, because if he had, October wouldn't have slept with him. And if she hadn't had slept with him, Minnow wouldn't have discovered them in bed and demand that Zeus terminate October's employment. Minnow's language had been far more colourful and far less Human Resources speak, and October still shuddered at the humiliation.

But the question on her mind now was, why did Zeus feel it necessary to inform her? Unless...

Her heart missed a beat and thumped uncomfortably to catch up, as she processed the information and arrived at a disconcerting conclusion; was he telling her this because he hoped October would return to his yard? But if that was the case, why didn't he simply say so?

Although, even if he begged her, she had no intention of going back to him. He'd hurt her, and she would be extremely wary of putting herself in a position where she could be hurt again.

October's stomach churned and she pulled a face, confusion clouding her mind. She missed her life in Kent terribly. She missed the horses, the rhythm of a showjumping yard, the other grooms, and the excitement and busyness of preparing for and going to an event.

But did she miss **Zeus**?

He was a brilliant rider – Olympic gold medal standard – and his was a face everyone in the showjumping world, and many not in it, would recognise.

She wondered what he was doing, whether he was going to the qualifiers in Birmingham, or if he might be off to Germany at the end of next month. Which horses would he take? Which grooms?

Suddenly she had a yearning to be sitting in the living room in the grooms' house, drinking cheap wine and arguing over whose turn it was to wash the dishes.

And, just as suddenly, she understood it was no longer the life for her. She was getting too old for this. Although she missed the excitement and the camaraderie, she didn't miss the incredibly early starts, nor the hours spent travelling, nor having a place to call home. She'd been a groom (and a wannabe professional showjumper in her own right) for longer than she cared to remember, and it was clear now that she was never going to be snapped up by a trainer or an owner who spotted her potential and begged her to ride for them in international competitions.

The closest she would ever come to her dream, had been working for others in their quest for glory.

Was she bitter?

A little, perhaps.

But she was also realistic enough to know that although she might be a competent rider and a pretty good showjumper, she didn't have the same flair as Zeus Fernsby. Neither did she have his money. You needed both in order to make it in the world of showjumping, and now that she'd finally recognised that she had neither, it was time to reconsider her options and her future.

Going back to Zeus's yard in Kent wasn't an option, and he couldn't possibly feature in her future. Not only did she not fully trust him (he should have told her he and Minnow were taking another shot at their marriage) but she didn't feel nearly as heartsore now as she'd done when he'd sheepishly informed her that she had to leave. Looking back, although she'd been incredibly upset, she hadn't been **heartbroken,** which told her that she hadn't loved him, although she had been infatuated with him.

Had it been Zeus the man who had drawn her to him, or had it been Zeus the famous rider...? She suspected the latter, which explained why she felt reluctant to respond to his message.

Anyway, what was she supposed to say? Commiserations? Congratulations? Well done?

October didn't like Minnow and Minnow most definitely didn't like October, but Minnow and Zeus made a striking couple. They were both tall, slim and athletic, with cut-glass accents and bags of style and confidence. Zeus had the talent, Minnow had the money. He had the fame, she had the connections and knew the right people. They looked good together.

They looked like they **belonged** together.

Although October was tall (like Minnow), slender (like Minnow) and had long, dark hair (like Minnow), that was where any similarity ended, and October knew when she was outclassed and outgunned.

Not only that, she suspected that Minnow still loved Zeus, and October would never forget the pain in the woman's eyes when she'd—

Enough of that! she told herself. There was no point in dwelling on the past. What was done, was done, and it couldn't be changed. She had to put it behind her and concentrate on her future – whatever that might look like. The only thing she was certain of was that she wanted to continue to work with horses; she couldn't imagine a life without them. But as for any non-horsey aspects such as romance, she still had no idea...

She did have another date with Luca this evening, though, and as unexpected as it was, she welcomed it. It would help take her mind of Zeus, and Luca **was** rather handsome, even if he was a bit smooth.

October chuckled as she thought about how he'd come a cropper when he'd attempted to show off his jumping skills, and how he'd bowed to her superior ability. It had been sweet and rather endearing. He'd taken his humiliation on the chin, and she respected him for it. And she'd enjoyed last night. He'd been good company – funny, humble, interesting, and his attention had been unwavering.

Zeus had ended his message with "Call me" (which she had no intention of doing) but before she put Zeus out of her mind once and for all, she gave in to the temptation to check the internet. He was a famous guy and there was bound to be some info about what he'd been getting up to recently.

She'd steadfastly avoided doing so until now, but curiosity finally got the better of her (and maybe there was a bit of prodding-at-a-loose-tooth about it, too) so she scrolled and clicked until she found a story reporting that his and Minnow's reconciliation had been short-lived and had ended acrimoniously, due to him being seen on the arm of another woman.

October took a deep breath and sincerely hoped **she** wasn't the other woman the article was referring to. She might have fallen for Zeus's undoubted charm, but she'd only allowed herself to do so because she'd believed that his marriage was well and truly over. There was no way she would have wanted to be responsible for Minnow's heartache.

Oh god, there was even a photo of October and him—

Hang on...**it wasn't her**.

October scrutinised it closely. It wasn't Minnow, either, although the woman in the photo had long dark hair, just like October herself.

Huh, Zeus had a type and this was it. The woman in the photo had her back to the camera and was leaning into Zeus, and from the tilt of her head October guessed she was looking up at him. Zeus had one hand on her bottom, cupping a buttock. His left hand. And his wedding ring was conspicuously absent from the third finger.

The article stated that these two had been seen together at an event which had taken place a mere ten days after October left his yard.

He hadn't wasted any time, had he?

October wondered who she could be.

It was rather telling that she felt nothing but distaste when she looked at Zeus, and pity welled up in her mind for Minnow. October and Zeus had both wronged her. However, October's sin against Minnow had been unwitting; Zeus had no such excuse.

Feeling rather grubby about the situation, October switched her phone off and threw it on the bed. She refused to give Zeus Fernsby any more headspace. It was time she put the whole thing behind her once and for all, and stopped lamenting her misfortune. She needed to concentrate on her future – whatever it might be. And the first step along the path to a new life was her date with Luca.

It might not come to anything (in fact, it probably wouldn't) but he intrigued her and she simply knew she was going to enjoy getting to know him better.

Luca hadn't gone ice skating in years, but he'd been rather good at it once. Good enough not to make a total fool of himself on the ice and fall over every five seconds. He used to be able to go backwards and do a twirl, and he wondered if he'd remember the technique – whether it was like falling off a bike and your muscles never truly forgot and all that was needed was a gentle reminder, or whether he'd be like Bambi, all legs and comedic expression.

He also wondered how well October skated, and he had a feeling she might be pretty good at it considering the alacrity with which she'd accepted the challenge.

It was going to be fun finding out, and he took his own advice and put a spare pair of jeans on the backseat of his car, just in case he spent more time on his bottom than he anticipated. Sitting in a restaurant with wet jeans wouldn't be pleasant.

But when he saw what she was carrying as she got into the passenger seat, he groaned. 'I might have known,' he said slapping the palm of his hand against his forehead. 'You own your own skates.'

'Yep. See 'em and weep, skater-boy.' She grinned at him, and he couldn't help grinning back.

He said, 'Shall we forgo the skating part and head straight for the restaurant, because you're clearly going to win this challenge.'

'And miss seeing you fall over? Not a chance.' She leaned towards him and he caught the subtle scent of her perfume. It made his mouth go dry with desire. 'I'll let you into a secret,' she said. 'I haven't skated since I was a teen. I'm surprised these still fit. When I told my mum where I was going this afternoon, she said my ice skates were still in the attic. Even if they no longer fitted me, it was worth bringing them just to see your expression.'

'You horrid person.'

'I am, aren't I?' she replied cheerfully. 'I'll be even more horrid when I beat you, and no cheating by hanging onto my coat and making me fall over. That's a foul, and will count as a fall on your part.'

'I would never do that. I play fair and square. No cheating.'

He was true to his word, despite October being a better skater than him. It was a pleasure to watch her on the ice once she'd regained her confidence. He was rather wobbly at first, too, but gradually he rediscovered his balance and practiced a few moves, and after a couple of topples he managed to remain upright.

There was one occasion where he came perilously close to running straight over a child who'd fallen right in front of him, but October grabbed his arm and yanked him towards her and he stumbled past the kid, his arms windmilling until she dragged him into the side.

'Close call,' he said. 'Thanks.'

'I didn't want a great big lump like you landing on top of that boy. Mind you, if I wasn't winning, I might have let you fall flat on your face.'

'And risk ruining these good looks?' he teased, pointing to his face, which was probably red and sweaty from the exertion.

October reached up to stroke his cheek, and Luca's heart skipped a beat as she gazed into his eyes. 'Roughing you up a bit might be a good idea,' she murmured.

'Oh?'

'You're far too attractive for your own good.'

Luca was stumped for a reply. He wanted to come back with something witty, but all he could think of was that she thought he was attractive. Lord, he wanted to kiss her: a deep, soul-searching kiss that would rock him to his core.

Then the mood was broken as she pushed off from the side and darted away.

He watched her go, admiring her grace. That wasn't all he was admiring though, as his gaze was captured by the way her hair flowed from side to side with each long, languid glide, her slim legs, and her rounded bottom encased in jeans which were free of tell-tale damp patches because she'd not fallen over once yet.

With a whoop, he chased after her.

When he caught her he had a feeling it might be a while before he let her go.

'What about you? Are you likely to stay in Picklewick?' Luca asked, and October considered the question as she picked up a piece of fried chicken and bit into it.

'I honestly don't know. I've been a stable hand or groom all my working life. I don't know what else I can do.' Or what else she wanted to do. Horses were all she knew.

'You like working at the stables on Muddypuddle Lane, though?'

She nodded, licking her fingers. They were in one of the fast-food places adjacent to the ice-rink, because October hadn't wanted to bother with a restaurant. She knew she was easily pleased but she was hungry **now** and she didn't want to have to drive somewhere, then wait for her food. Luca had argued that as he was paying (he'd lost the bet) he should be the one to choose and he'd wanted to take her to a nice place and wine and dine her. But she'd got her own way, and now he was happily tucking into his bucket of chicken as enthusiastically as he would have tucked into a cordon-bleu meal.

'I do like it,' she said. 'Petra is lovely, but I'm not sure I can see myself working there for the rest of my life. It's meant to be a stop-gap until I sort something else out.' She wasn't sure how much she should share with him, but neither did she want him to think she was staying in Picklewick permanently. If she intended to work for another professional rider, she'd have no choice other than to leave Picklewick.

'What do you want to do?' he asked, licking his own fingers, and she tried not to focus on his mouth and the way it made her feel.

'I have no idea,' she replied, honestly. 'When I was younger, my dream was to become a famous showjumper and ride in competitions all over the world. But I'm thirty now, and I realise that's never going to happen. Don't get me wrong,' she added, in case he thought she was bitter about it. 'I've loved travelling to different places and caring for wonderful horses, but it can be hard. Stable hands often move from yard to yard, and it can be a very unsettled life. I suppose I could have bought a house and stayed in one location and in one job, but I was chasing my dream for such a long time that it took being—' She stopped, wondering if she should tell him the whole story.

'Being what?' he asked, wiping his lips with a serviette.

'Every job I've had, I was either renting a room in a house or living in the accommodation provided for the grooms. Either way, I was sharing with other staff, and barely earning enough to have my hair cut twice a year. When accommodation and utilities are provided as part of the job, the wages are often considerably less than they would otherwise be.'

'I can see how that might happen,' Luca said. 'But now you're ready for a change?'

'I want to have a place of my own someday, to get married and have kids,' she said. 'I suppose being sacked from my last job has acted as a kind of catalyst. It made me re-evaluate my life.'

'Oh, dear. What happened? You don't have to tell me if you don't want to,' he added, reaching out to briefly squeeze her hand.

She wanted to tell him though, so she took a deep breath. 'I was working for this guy called Zeus Fernsby. He was married and we had a relationship, but not until he and his wife had split up. What he'd failed to tell me, was that they had decided to make another go of it.

Minnow, his wife, caught us in bed together. I lost my job and my home, so I've moved in with my mum for a while.'

'That's awful,' he said. 'But I'm glad you came to Picklewick.'

So was October. It was time she seriously thought about what she intended to do with the rest of her life, and a teeny, tiny part of her was beginning to hope Luca might feature somewhere in her future.

'What about you – do you want to do the wife and children bit one day?' she asked.

'Definitely.' He became sombre. 'I thought I was close to that once or twice, but it didn't work out. I've had a few disastrous relationships in the past. The women I've dated see the money, not me; which is daft, because although I might own my own company I'm not exactly rich.'

'False advertising,' she said, sipping the dregs of her drink through a straw.

'I'm sorry?'

'So you should be – you drive an Aston Martin, you wear expensive clothes and you take girls to posh restaurants.'

Luca glanced around. 'I don't call this posh,' he laughed.

'It's not where you planned on taking me, is it?'

He shrugged. 'I suppose not.'

'There you go, then. Women see all that and think you're rich.'

He stared into space. 'You're right. Should I ditch the car?'

'I'd ditch the women. You could always borrow Petra's old Land Rover and take your dates to a fast-food place. That would weed the gold-diggers from the ones who genuinely like you.'

'Excellent advice. On that note, what do you think of the food here, and would you consider another date? Or has eating fries and greasy chicken out of a cardboard box put you off me?'

'I think I'll give another date a try. How about a burger van, next time? Or fish and chips out of paper?' She was only half-joking – she rather liked a fish and chip supper.

'I want to kiss you.'

Oh. Okay, she was good with that. More than good, as her leaping heart indicated, and when they returned to the car and he kissed her, October had no hesitation in twining her arms around his neck and pulling him close.

Initially, when his lips found hers their kiss was soft and gentle, but when she opened her mouth to let him in, and she tasted him and felt his tongue play with hers, she uttered a moan of longing.

Deepening the kiss, he held her tight, one hand on the small of her back, the other buried in her hair, and she lost herself in the exquisite sensations washing over her. The feel of him, the taste, his scent, his soft groan as he clasped her to him – all of it made her head spin and her pulse race.

Finally she drew back, pulling away gradually, his lips following to trail kisses down the side of her neck until she shivered with longing.

'I'd better take you home,' he said, even though the night was still young.

And although she was grateful for his restraint, what she really wanted to do was to take him to bed.

Thank goodness one of them could control themselves she thought, because after that marvellous, wonderful, mind-blowing kiss, October wasn't sure she could trust herself to behave around him. Oh, boy...

CHAPTER FOUR

'Are you sure you're happy riding Hercules?' Petra asked as October saddled the stallion under Petra's watchful eye. 'I'd take him out myself but I've got an architect coming to look at the cowshed.'

October grinned. 'I can't wait,' she said. Hercules was an ex-racehorse and could be a handful on occasion, but she'd ridden much more highly strung animals than this one.

'You will be careful with him?' Petra looked anxious and October hurried to reassure her.

'I will,' she promised. Hercules was Petra's horse, her pride and joy, and October felt honoured that Petra was trusting her with him.

He hadn't been ridden for the best part of a week, and he had shied and bucked a bit when October had placed the saddle cloth on his back and he'd realised he was going to have to work for his keep.

'Luca should be here any minute,' Petra said, and October gave her a sharp look.

'Okay...?'

'Didn't I mention that he was going for a ride this morning?' Petra's face was a picture of false innocence, and October bristled.

'It's not that I don't think you can handle Hercules,' Petra continued, swiftly. 'I thought you might like some company, and as he was already taking Midnight for a hack, I thought the two of you could go out together. It's always more fun when you have company.'

October shook her head in disbelief. 'You're matchmaking,' she accused. She knew full well that Petra liked nothing more than being out on the moors on her own, just her and her horse.

'I think the matchmaking has already been done, don't you?' Petra replied with a knowing smirk.

October felt her cheeks grow warm, and she bent her head to check the girth in order to hide her face. She and Luca's relationship wasn't a secret, but it was so new, she wasn't entirely sure it actually **was** a relationship. What they had was a couple of dates and a toe-curling scintillating kiss.

Oh, that kiss...

'Speak of the devil,' Petra said, and October looked around to see Luca leading Midnight into the barn.

The horses whickered a greeting. Petra beamed.

October and Luca shot each other shy smiles, and October wondered whether Luca was thinking about the other night. She certainly was. She hadn't been able to get him out of her mind. They had another date arranged for this Saturday, but she hadn't expected to see him midweek even though she knew that he popped up to the stables regularly to check on his horse, so this was an unexpected and very welcome pleasure.

'I'll leave you to it,' Petra said, sauntering out of the barn.

'She seems rather pleased with herself,' Luca observed.

'We've been set up.' October placed her foot in the stirrup and swung herself onto Hercules's back.

A look of confusion spread across his face. 'Did we **need** setting up? I thought we were... um...?'

'Are we?' October wasn't sure, either.

'Going steady, you mean?'

'Er, yeah...'

'I thought we were. I know nothing's been said, but...'

October bit back a smile. Neither of them was capable of completing a sentence, it seemed. 'I assumed...' she said.

'So did I.'

'That we are? Or we aren't?' October wanted to know.

'Would you like to? I mean please don't feel obliged. I've kind of put you on the spot. Sorry.' Luca wore an anxious expression.

'Don't be – I'm not. And yes, I would like to "go steady".'

'That's fantastic! I could kiss you.' He gave her a big grin.

'Later,' she said.

'Is that a promise?'

'It is.' She nodded, catching hold of her bottom lip with her teeth, a shiver of excitement surging over her.

The desire in his eyes made her tummy lurch and she looked away, certain that her own rising passion was written all over her face.

Goodness, all they'd done was banter and she was already shaken and unbalanced.

As if sensing her mood, Hercules pawed the ground and snorted. She pulled his head up and he arched his neck and pranced to the side.

'I think he's eager to get going,' October said.

Luca seemed to blink and shake himself, and she wondered what he'd been thinking, and whether it was as wicked as her own thoughts. As far as she was concerned later couldn't come soon enough.

When Petra had informed him that Hercules needed to be exercised and that she was going to ask October to take him out, Luca had wondered how it concerned him. But on being told that Hercules could be a loose cannon and that Petra would feel happier if October had someone with her, Luca didn't hesitate in offering to go on a hack with her.

It was only when he arrived at the stables that he understood October hadn't needed anyone to accompany her after all.

He should have realised – October was an exceptionally competent rider, better than Petra, and she would have been perfectly fine hacking alone, which Petra already knew.

October was right, they **had** been set up.

Petra didn't realise that they'd already been on two dates and had another lined up for the weekend. Luca wasn't complaining about seeing October today, though; he was positively delighted and he couldn't stop grinning.

She looked delectable, all muffled up in a scarf, thick coat and gloves. She even wore a pair of earmuffs over the top of her helmet and he had a sudden urge to lift one of the fluffy pads and nibble the exposed ear.

Hastily, he cleared his throat and mounted Midnight. It wouldn't do to be having such delicious thoughts when they were about to venture onto the wild and windy moors. It was January and freezing, so there was a fair chance his ardour would be dampened long before they returned to the stables.

It was certainly fresh outside, he decided, as the pair of them made their way along the track next to the fields leading onto the hills above the stables. But there were already hints of spring, and he ducked as dangling catkins from several overhanging branches tickled his cheek. Tiny buds could be seen on an old oak tree, waiting to unfurl, and although the ground beneath was mostly bare, Luca noticed vibrant green shoots poking their heads through the soil.

He also became aware of birdsong; the cheeps and chirps of sparrows in the hedgerow, the trilling voice of a blackbird high in a tree, and there was the unmistakable silhouette of a bird of prey overhead. The land was coming back to life, slowly and surely, and before long spring would be here. The knowledge made his heart sing.

He found he was looking forward to riding with October when the weather was warmer. Maybe they could bring a picnic and a blanket? They could tether the horses, and lay the blanket down in a grassy, secluded spot—

Flippin' heck, he was getting ahead of himself, wasn't he? They'd only just agreed they were a couple and he was already planning trysts in the open air – which made him realise that he was hoping their relationship would continue to grow.

He couldn't wait to kiss her again.

'October? Can we get off for a minute?'

October was ahead of him as the horses were walking in single file, and she glanced over her shoulder, a look of concern on her face. 'Sure. Is anything wrong?'

Luca reined Midnight in and slid off his back. He waited for her to dismount, then said, 'Come here and loop the reins over that gate.' His voice was husky and his heart was thumping. He tethered his own horse and waited, his mouth dry, his pulse racing.

She came towards him, her attention on Midnight. 'Is he okay?'

'He's fine.'

'Are you—? **Ohhh.**' She let out her breath in a soft sigh as he caught her around the waist, pulled her to him, and covered her mouth with his.

Her lips were cold and she tasted of fresh air and the lip salve she wore. He could smell apples in her hair, and coconut and vanilla on her skin, and she felt firm yet soft against his chest as she kissed him back with passion.

It was October who withdrew first – Luca could have carried on kissing her all day.

'As lovely as this is,' she said, 'those horses aren't getting much exercise. And it's cold!'

'I can keep you warm,' he said, raising his eyebrows suggestively, and she batted him on the arm.

'I bet you could. Behave yourself.'

'Spoilsport.'

'That's me. Now, get back on your horse. Race you to the top?' She gestured towards the track. It had widened and levelled off somewhat, but there was a gradual gradient rising to the top of the moor.

Without waiting for a reply, she wriggled free of him and dashed towards Hercules. Startled, the horse jerked his head up, and was already prancing in anticipation as October leapt onto his back. She turned him to face the right way and then she was off, leaving Luca staring after her and shaking his head in disbelief.

Realising he was being left behind, he followed, urging Midnight into a canter. 'Not fair,' he shouted. 'He's a damned racehorse.'

'**Ex** racehorse,' she called back, and her laughter floated in the air.

Whooping, he raced after her, his own laughter bubbling up. When he caught her he'd kiss her so thoroughly she'd be begging for mercy. **If** he caught her...

Damn, she was good!

But when he did eventually catch her (he rather suspected she had let him) neither of them felt the cold for quite some time.

'I'll be in touch as soon as I have some outline plans drawn up,' Isaac Richards said, shaking Petra's hand. 'If you're happy with them, I'll leave a copy with you to use as a basic guide for builders to give you a quote. After that, if you decide you definitely want to go ahead with the build, let me know and I'll draw up more detailed ones for you to submit to the planning department for approval.'

Petra blew out a breath, her cheeks ballooning. 'It's complicated, isn't it?'

'Yes, but I'll guide you through it.'

She saw him back to his car and as he drove off down the lane, she sighed. Even the outline plans were costing money she didn't have, but there was no point in doing this half-heartedly. And for her to have a more accurate picture of how much it was going to cost, she needed to obtain several quotes for the build, and even then Isaac had advised her that she'd need to set aside a contingency fund of twenty per cent on top.

Petra returned to the office and the copious notes she'd made, and she was busy filing them away, her mind full of partition walls and skylight windows, when the phone rang.

'Do you have a woman by the name of October Rees working for you?' The voice on the other end was female and had an accent that would put the royal family to shame.

Petra wasn't impressed. 'What's it to you?'

'Do you, or don't you?'

'As I said, what's it to you?'

Petra wasn't in the mood for this, although she was glad to have an excuse to think about something other than the blasted cowshed, because all this conversion stuff was giving her a headache. Crossly, she rubbed her eyes.

'My name is Minnow Fernsby. I assume you've heard of my husband.'

'If he's Zeus Fernsby, I've already spoken to him.' Was this woman calling about October's reference? If so, she was wasting her time – Zeus Fernsby had provided one.

'So she **does** work for you,' the woman cried. 'Because there couldn't possibly be any other reason for my husband to speak to **you**. He gave her a reference, didn't he?'

Petra didn't say anything.

Minnow took Petra's silence for confirmation, and continued, 'Did he tell you he had to **let her go**—' Minnow emphasised the words '—because she seduced him? That's right, she **seduced** my husband. She's untrustworthy and duplicitous. What I mean by that is, she's deceitful and treacherous.'

'I know what duplicitous means,' Petra said through gritted teeth. Just who did this woman think she was? 'And I don't care.'

'You will when she leaves you in the lurch.'

'What do you mean?'

'She's not going to hang around in a little riding school for kiddies, is she? Not now.'

'What. Do. You. Mean?' Petra was a hair's breadth from hanging up on Minnow Fernsby, and she would have done so if she hadn't needed to know whether October was actually about to hand in her notice. Petra didn't think she could face going through the rigmarole of advertising and interviewing again.

'She's been seen with him,' Minnow spat.

'Who?'

'My **husband**, who do you think? He told me he'd ended it, that he'd sacked her, but it's all over the internet. So you can tell her from me, she's welcome to him.' The woman let out a sob, and even though she was possibly the most annoying person Petra had come across since a delightful parent by the name of Cher had told her how to run the stables and had then set her sights on Harry, Petra felt sorry for her.

'She can have him,' Minnow continued. 'Much good it will do her. Let's see how the pair of them like living on fresh air. And you can tell her that from me, too.'

And with that she abruptly ended the call, leaving Petra wondering whether she should expect a letter of resignation from October, and if so how the hell was she going to manage.

Working at the stables on Muddypuddle Lane was turning out to be much more fun than October would ever have imagined. For one thing, she'd discovered that she enjoyed teaching kids how to ride, and she was happy to split her working day in order to take a class or two in the evening. It meant coming in early to muck out and do any other jobs, then go back home, only to have to return later; but she didn't mind. And for another, she wouldn't have met Luca if it wasn't for this job.

It was quite telling that Zeus had never made her feel quite as giddy as Luca was making her feel. Admittedly, she'd had her head turned by him, but he hadn't had the effect on her that Luca was having, like a hormone-driven teenager with a major crush.

October was singing **I Will Survive** to herself under her breath and making up the buckets of grain ready for this evening, when Petra appeared in the doorway of the feed store.

'Can I have a word?' she asked, and October immediately stopped what she was doing.

'Of course.' She wiped her hands on the backside of her breeches and looked at Petra expectantly, hoping she hadn't done anything wrong.

Petra leaned against the doorjamb and folded her arms. 'I've just had a woman by the name of Minnow Fernsby on the phone,' she began.

October's good mood abruptly fled.

'What did she want?' She could kind of guess... Had she phoned to warn Petra not to leave any stray husbands lying around? To tell her new employer that she was a homewrecker? October felt sorry for Minnow, but if the woman wanted to lay any blame for the breakup of her marriage, it should be at her husband's door.

'To tell me you were going to leave me in the lurch,' Petra stated.

'Excuse me? Why on earth would she think that?'

'Because she claimed that you and her husband are back together. Is it true?'

'It most definitely is not! I can't think where she's got that idea from—' October froze. Oh, yes, she could. 'Hang on.' She fished her phone out of the pocket of her breeches. 'Here,' she said, after a moment, turning it around so Petra could see the screen.

Petra squinted at it. 'Is that you?'

'No. The photo was taken ten days after I left his yard; it couldn't be me because I was here in Picklewick having an interview with you.'

'He likes women with long dark hair, does he?' Petra said.

'He most certainly does. His wife has got long hair too, but hers has some grey in it now. I get the feeling he's trying to trade her in for a younger model.'

'That old cliché?'

October nodded. 'I feel rather sorry for her. She can be quite obnoxious, but she doesn't deserve to be treated like that. She should kick him into touch.'

Petra smirked. 'I think that's what she intends to do. She mentioned something about him living on fresh air?'

Good for her, October thought. Zeus deserved what was coming to him. She was well out of it, and hopefully that was the last she'd hear from Zeus or Minnow. She had a new life here, and it mightn't be the one she thought she'd be living when she first started her riding career, but she was surprised to discover she was happier now than she'd been for some considerable time.

Harry kissed Petra on the top of her head and sat down to supper. Goodie, sausage, mashed potatoes, and rich onion gravy; he was ravenous. Being outside all day in the cold did that to him, despite the heat his portable forge kicked out.

'I met with an architect today,' Petra said, poking a fork at the sausages on her plate.

'I wondered who you were holed up in the office with,' Amos said. 'Are we going ahead with it?' He pushed the dish of mash across the table. Petra ignored it.

'I doubt it. I didn't realise how many rules and regulations there are when it comes to converting an old building, and the cowshed isn't even a listed one. And the health and safety stuff alone is enough to make me cry.'

'That's the responsibility of the builder, isn't it? Speaking of builders, have you asked anyone to give us a quote yet?' Amos tucked into his food with enthusiasm.

'Not yet. Isaac – that's the architect – said he'd draw up some plans so the builder could give us a more accurate quote.'

Around a mouthful of food Harry said, 'I thought you were going to get a ballpark figure first?'

'I was, but when I looked into it, I realised we need to know what we can and can't do with the shed first. There's no point in asking for a quote for three cottages if the configuration and the available space means we can only have two.' She sighed deeply.

As he listened to Petra speak, Harry smiled fondly; she was already sounding as though she knew what she was talking about, which was impressive considering she hated admin and paperwork with a passion.

'Do you want me to step in?' he offered. 'I don't mind meeting architects and dealing with builders.'

She shook her head. 'Thanks, Harry, but this is down to me and Amos.'

He heard the subtle hint that although he lived at the stables the business wasn't his responsibility. Which was fair enough — he had no financial interest or say in the stables, and he fully understood that if any decisions were to be made, Amos and Petra had to make them. Actually, it was **Amos's** decision, because he was the one who owned the stables and he would be the one who would have to raise the funds needed.

Harry wished he could do something to help. Coming up with ideas was all well and good, but from where he was sitting he seemed to have added to Petra's burden, not lightened it.

She looked as though she had the weight of the world on her shoulders. If only he could help out more…

Suddenly he knew what he could do, and once the idea lodged in his mind, he instinctively knew how right it was, how perfect.

Harry was going to ask Petra to marry him.

CHAPTER FIVE

Petra inhaled deeply and squared her shoulders. She could do this. It was only for an hour – more like an hour and a half in reality by the time she'd chatted to those parents to didn't seem to have homes to go to. Nathan, bless him, had saddled up all the ponies that would be needed for this evening's lesson and they were waiting patiently in the arena for their riders to arrive.

Thankfully this was an intermediate class, and the pupils would be concentrating on the finer controls of horse handling, such as asking their mount to lead on alternate legs and getting them to back up nicely and without fuss.

She didn't think she could face an energetic lesson over jumps, or one where they played games. Petra was so tired she didn't know what to do with herself. Neither did it help that she felt bloated and completely out of sorts. And her jodhpurs were too tight because Amos had managed to shrink them in the wash. God knows what cycle he was using on that blasted washing machine. She was tempted to do her own laundry, but she knew her uncle would be hurt if she suggested it. Since the onset of his angina, the arrangement was that he took care of the paperwork and all the household chores, whilst she concentrated on running the stables. It usually worked well, but not when it came to a new washing machine and her clothes. He'd even managed to shrink her bras, because every single one felt uncomfortable, as though she was spilling out of them.

At least, that was what she told herself – she didn't want to acknowledge that the

apparent shrinking of various garments
was probably more to do with the fact
she was eating like a horse lately, so had
put on weight.

It was because of the cold weather, she
told herself as she bent over awkwardly
to stuff her feet into her Wellington boots.
It always made her hungry, and what
with being outdoors so much she was
bound to burn more calories at this time
of year, therefore it was only to be
expected that she ate more to
compensate.

One by one her students arrived, and the
next few minutes were a flurry of saying
hello to everyone, asking how they'd
been, listening to tales of what the kids
had got up to in the week since she'd
seen them last.

Finally they'd all arrived and were
mounted up, and she could get on with
the lesson. She usually enjoyed teaching,
but lately it had become more of a chore

and she would be glad when the time came for the little darlings to go home. Not only was she shattered, but she didn't have much patience. They were all so loud and boisterous, and she didn't know how their parents put up with them. Which was one of the reasons why today's lesson featured the basics of dressage – it took concentration and therefore would hopefully keep them quiet.

Trying to remain focused (it would be so unfair on her young riders for her not to give them her best), Petra studied her pupils, providing each one with feedback and encouragement. One girl, Heidi Walker, had reached the limit with this class. She needed to move to the next one where she'd be challenged more, and Petra made a mental note to remember to ask her to stay behind after the lesson so she could have a chat with the girl's mum. Heidi had the talent, the enthusiasm and the dedication to make a competent rider, and Petra wanted to encourage that.

'Can I have a quick word?' Petra said to Heidi's mum, Rose, when the lesson finally drew to a close.

Petra was supervising the dismounting process, encouraging her charges to shorten stirrup straps and loosen girths so she didn't have to, under the guise of trying to teach them some basic horse care, whilst being relieved that it was one less job she had to do herself.

A frown creased Rose's forehead, and Petra hastened to add, 'It's nothing to worry about. I just wanted to chat about Heidi's progress.' Mindful that the child's mum mightn't want Heidi to move up a class (it was on a different day and at a different time, so it might not be convenient) Petra said to Heidi, 'Do you think you could take your pony and May's to their stables? You're sensible enough and Nathan is there to give you a hand if you need it. Is that okay with you, Rose?'

Thank goodness Nathan had agreed to stay on for a while – Petra would have had to have spent at least another hour bedding the ponies down for the night if she'd had to do it all by herself. She'd debated whether to ask October, but she had a hunch her new employee may have had plans with Luca.

Rose followed Petra into the office and Petra slumped against the desk, gesturing for her to sit down.

'I see congratulations are in order,' Petra said, nodding to the woman's gently swelling stomach. She hadn't realised Rose was pregnant until just now.

Rose smiled and rubbed her belly. 'It was a bit unexpected,' she said. 'Neither Jason nor I had talked about having more children, but once we'd got over the shock, we're both delighted.'

Petra thought about the family's dynamics – they were each a single parent with a daughter, and both had custody of their child. Rose and Jason had met at the stables, and Petra had watched their romance unfold over the course of the previous summer.

'How does Heidi and May feel about the new baby?' Petra asked, wondering if she needed to keep a weather eye on any potential behaviour issues in class.

'They're thrilled. They want a brother, but I've told them they don't get to choose.' She paused for a moment, then said, 'It's going to be a pain bringing a baby along to the riding lessons, but I want to try to keep things as normal as possible so the girls don't feel pushed out.'

Petra was about to say that the reason she'd asked for a chat was to discuss Heidi's lessons when Rose said, 'You'll have to start a creche. Or is Amos going to look after your little one when it arrives?'

'Excuse me?'

'I'm sorry, I didn't mean to speak out of turn. You're starting to show, so I thought...' Rose trailed off, and colour flooded her cheeks. 'Oh, dear.'

'I'm not pregnant,' Petra said.

Rose bit her lip. 'I'm sorry,' she repeated. She was clearly mortified.

'We've got a new washing machine and I've been eating like a horse, and...' It was Petra's turn to grind to a halt, as what Rose said took root. 'You don't think...?'

She glanced down at her tummy in shock. Surely it was only protruding a bit because she was slouched against the desk and was hunched over slightly?

'Oh, shoot.' Petra closed her eyes, her heart dropping to her wellies. She couldn't be. **Could she**?

Conscious that she wasn't alone in the office, Petra opened them again to see Rose's concerned and knowing gaze fixed firmly on her.

Abruptly everything made sense: her dreadful exhaustion, her increased appetite, her sore boobs, the way her clothes were too snug, the fact that she hadn't had a period in god knows how long. How could she have failed to notice?

'Didn't you realise?' Rose asked gently, and Petra shook her head.

She felt like crying. How could this have happened? She pulled a face – she knew **how**, obviously, but... Damn. She wasn't ready for this. Babies weren't on her agenda. They never had been. She wasn't the motherly type. Harry had never mentioned it; the subject hadn't come up. She'd just assumed that after being both mother and father to Timothy for so many years since the brothers lost their mum and dad in an accident when Timothy was eleven, Harry would have had enough of parenting.

Petra briefly closed her eyes again. Harry...she'd have to tell him.

Dear Lord, what was she going to do? How would they manage? The riding school was barely hanging on by its fingernails without **this**.

She was scarcely aware of Rose leaving, and when she did notice she was tempted to run after her and beg her not to mention anything to anyone. Because it mightn't be true. Petra prayed it wasn't. She didn't want a baby. And neither did Harry.

But what if it was?

She'd only just found Harry. Their love was not even a year old. How would he take it? Would he still want her once she told him her news?

The thought that he might not sent fingers of ice clutching at her heart.

'Petra? Amos?' Harry almost fell through the front door in his haste to get out of the wind and the rain. 'Anyone home?'

'I'm in the kitchen,' Amos shouted, so that was where Harry headed.

'Is Petra around?' he asked, relishing the warmth as he entered the room.

'She's in the arena – got a class.'

'What time does the lesson finish?'

Amos glanced at the clock on the mantelpiece. One of the things Harry loved about the former farmhouse was the open fireplaces in all the downstairs rooms. The one in the kitchen wasn't lit very often because the Aga kicked out so much heat, but today a fire smouldered and two dogs and a cat were sprawled on the rug in front of it.

'Any minute now, I think. How about you? Are you done for the day?' Amos asked.

'Yes, thank goodness. It's freezing out there. Farmyards and stables are the coldest, draftiest places on the planet.'

Patch, Nathan's little Jack Russell terrier, lifted his head before flopping back down again, and Queenie, Petra's spaniel, wagged her tail but otherwise didn't move. The cat ignored him. He walked over to the fire, careful not to step on any paws or tails, and crouched down, holding out his hands to the flames.

Harry stayed there for a moment, gathering his courage. He wanted to ask

Amos a question but it could only be asked when Petra wasn't in earshot, so right now was the ideal time as long as he was quick. He didn't want to risk her coming in at the wrong moment.

However, Harry was fretting that Amos would think it was too soon for such a big step, or that the old fella wouldn't want him for a son-in-law. Not that Petra was Amos's daughter – she was his niece – but to Harry she felt more Amos's child than her real father did. He'd only met her dad once and it had been an awkward affair; the two men hadn't connected and had found little in common.

So if he intended to ask anyone's permission to marry Petra, he was going to ask Amos.

'Er, can I ask you something?' he said. 'It's important.'

'Ask away,' Amos replied. He was rolling out pastry for an apple tart, the contents of which were in a bowl, cooling.

Harry straightened up and turned to face him. The question was far too momentous to be asked in a crouching position. He took a deep breath, held it for a second, then let it out slowly.

'I'd like to ask for Petra's hand in marriage,' he said. He knew it was an old-fashioned thing to do, but he wanted to do things properly. Petra deserved it.

Amos's back stiffened. He stopped what he was doing, put the rolling pin on the counter and turned around.

Harry felt a degree of relief that at least Amos wasn't about to brain him with it. Crikey, he was more nervous about this than he had been when Petra had asked Amos if he'd minded Harry moving in. Petra might run the stables, but it was

Amos who owned it, and he had the ultimate say in who lived in his house.

Amos narrowed his eyes and studied him, saying nothing. He might have an air of a friendly Captain Birdseye about him with his weather-beaten face, crinkly eyes and almost white beard, but he was no pushover and Harry wondered what he was thinking.

Slowly Amos nodded. 'Yes, on one condition.'

Anything, Harry thought. If Amos wanted him to sign a prenup, he'd willingly do so.

'I'd like Petra to wear my wife's engagement ring. It's Petra's by rights and I know her aunt would have wanted her to have it.'

Harry almost sagged with relief. 'It will be an honour, and I know Petra will feel the same.' He was touched that the elderly gent felt so strongly about it. It must hold great sentimental value, and instinctively Harry knew it was the right thing to do.

'Wait there, I'll fetch it,' Amos said, swilling his hands under the tap and wiping them on a towel. He walked to the door and was nearly through it, when he hesitated. 'Welcome to the family, son. I know the pair of you will be very happy. You're made for each other.'

Harry believed so, too. He just hoped Petra felt the same way, because Harry was far from certain she'd say yes when he popped the question.

October wasn't the best cook in the world, and for some reason she hadn't expected Luca to be either. So when he'd casually mentioned he liked cooking, she'd suggested that instead of going out for a meal, he might like to make her something.

She hadn't missed the hunger in his eyes when he'd agreed, and she was well aware that food might not be the only thing on the menu this evening.

The thought made her go weak at the knees. Whenever she was with him, her pulse soared and her stomach knotted, and all she wanted to do was to kiss him and be held by him.

She'd had her fair share of boyfriends and she wasn't inexperienced when it came to the bedroom, but October could honestly say she'd never felt like this about any man. Not only did he make her feel faint from pure lust, but she also couldn't stop thinking about him, and although she wasn't in love with him yet, it was only a matter of time before she was head over heels.

The wonderful thing was, he seemed to feel the same way about her.

Therefore she could guess what he was hoping for this evening, but she also knew him well enough by now to realise that he wouldn't push her to go to bed with him, that he'd leave it to her to tell him when she was ready.

Oh, boy, was she ready!

She hadn't been able to think of anything else all day, so by the time she arrived on his doorstep, she was all a-fizz with anticipation.

'Nice place,' she said nonchalantly when Luca opened the door.

'It'll do,' he replied, just as casually, but when his eyes bored into hers she wasn't fooled. He was nervous, and the realisation excited her even more. It was also rather endearing, and she smiled to think he wasn't as cocky and as confident as he appeared. Mind you, she already knew that, because if he had been they would never have had a second date.

'What are we having?' she asked as he led her through the depths of his large house and into the kitchen. 'Wow! It's huge.'

October gazed around the open-plan room in amazement. The island in front of a row of cabinets was bigger than a tennis court (only a slight exaggeration, she felt), and the kitchen area merged into a dining space that could seat a football team, and then into a squashy sofa area with plate glass doors leading onto a terrace. If the house had been impressive from the outside, it was stunning inside.

'Is all this just for you?' she asked.

He nodded, ducking his head, but not before she'd glimpsed embarrassment on his face. 'This is my forever home,' he said. 'I'd like to raise a family here.'

'How many kids were you planning on having?' she cried, circling the huge table, and running her hand across its polished surface. 'I like the décor, by the way.'

'Thanks.'

'Did you get someone in to do it?' It wasn't terribly subtle of her, but she wanted to know if another woman had had a hand in it, and a prickle of jealousy niggled at her.

'All my own work,' he said.

'I can't see you trailing around kitchen showrooms,' she laughed, the green-eyed monster subsiding.

'Ah, but I did. I found it quite therapeutic.'

'That's not what my mum said, when she was looking for a new kitchen. This is lovely, by the way.'

'I'm glad you like it. And in answer to your question, we're having enchiladas.'

'Great! I'm starving.'

'Would you like a drink while I finish up here? If you want a glass of wine, I'll happily drive you home, then pick you up in the morning to fetch your car.'

'Are you trying to get me drunk so you can have your wicked way with me?'

'I wouldn't dare,' Luca replied, and he looked as though he meant it.

'Pity...'

His eyebrows shot up and he stared at her.

'I'll have a glass of wine,' she said,' but there's no need to drive me home.'

'Isn't there?'

Abruptly the air was super-charged and she found it difficult to breathe as a frisson of excitement made her shiver.

'No...' Her reply was slow, languid even, and she watched his eyes darken as her meaning became clear.

'Are you sure?'

It was sweet of him to ask. 'Totally.'

He cleared his throat but despite that his voice was rough and husky when he said, 'I'll fetch the wine.'

'Take me to bed first.' she said, and in two strides he was standing in front of her and scooping her up as though she weighed nothing.

'My pleasure,' he said.

But, as it turned out, the pleasure was as much hers as his. More so perhaps...

'Do you want that wine now?' Luca asked, easing his arm out from underneath her, and propping himself up on an elbow.

'I am rather thirsty after all that exercise,' October said, her tone teasing. 'Hungry, too.'

'Mmm, so am I.' Luca nibbled at that delectable spot where her neck and collarbone met. He'd quickly discovered the secret to driving her wild. One of them...

'Stop it,' she squealed, pushing him away. 'Let's eat, we've got all night.'

'In case you hadn't noticed, half the night has gone already.'

'Really?' October sat up and looked at the clock. 'So it has. It's amazing how time flies when you're enjoying yourself.'

Luca smirked. 'Glad to hear you had a good time.'

'I think you did, too.'

'Hell, yeah,' he breathed. He'd most definitely had a good time. The pair of them had fitted together perfectly, no awkwardness, no embarrassing moments – just pure harmony. And a deep connection. He'd had fantastic sex before, but it had always been on a physical level. Making love with October had touched his soul. And his heart.

He was falling for her hard, and whilst he was excited and thrilled, he was also scared – he'd never felt like this before and it was terrifying.

CHAPTER SIX

October risked another look at Petra out of the corner of her eye and wondered what was wrong. Petra, like Nathan, could be rather quiet, but this morning she was positively morose. The two of them were in the office, October giving the helmets a clean with disinfectant wipes and Petra leaning against the desk, staring into space

Was she unwell? She might be, because she kept rubbing her stomach. Maybe Petra had eaten something that didn't agree with her, or maybe her period had arrived and she had cramps?

No, that wasn't it. Petra didn't appear to be in pain. She appeared to be thoughtful, introspective—

October let out a gasp.

Petra was pregnant! October could definitely see a small bump, at odds with the woman's slim frame.

'Did you say something?' Petra asked.

'Please don't take this the wrong way, but are you pregnant?' October asked.

Petra snapped into focus and the glare she gave her made October wish she hadn't opened her mouth. 'What makes you say that?'

'Erm...nothing.' Oops, she'd gone and put her foot in it.

'I want to know.'

'You're...er...I thought you might be showing a bit.'

'Bugger.'

'You **are** pregnant? Congratulations! That's wonderful.'

'No, it's not.'

'Ah, I see.' October cast around for something to say. 'How far along are you?'

'I'm not sure.'

'Okay. They should be able to tell you when you have a scan.'

Petra pulled a face. 'What scan?'

'You usually have one at twelve weeks.' October saw Petra's expression. 'Your doctor should have explained it.'

'I haven't been to the doctor. I haven't even taken a test.' She swallowed and shook her head. 'I only realised yesterday that I might be pregnant.'

'Crumbs, you really do need to do a test,' October urged. 'If you don't mind me asking, when was your last period?'

'The middle of October. Ish. I can't honestly remember.'

'Okay...' October didn't know what to say to that; she religiously kept track of hers, especially when she had a boyfriend. Like now...

As if reading her mind, Petra said, 'I never needed to keep a record of them, they just happened.' She screwed up her face. 'I can't believe I didn't notice that I haven't had one since before Halloween. I've been so stupid.' She put her hands over her face and October's heart went out to her.

'I didn't think about it,' Petra continued, her voice muffled. 'It's been so busy, what with Harry moving in, and Faith selling Midnight, and all the extra work that caused. Then there was Christmas, and the horse rustling incident...' Petra straightened up, turned sideways and pulled her fleece taut across her midriff. There was a small, rounded bump below her belly button. 'I can't be more than twelve weeks, but I don't know how you work it out.'

'Um, I think you calculate it from the first day of your last period,' October said. One of the grooms had found out she was pregnant last year and had shared all the details.

'Wait a minute.' Petra sat down at the desk and flipped through the diary, her mouth a thin line. 'There, that's when it was!' She jabbed a finger at the page. 'I remember because the kids were about to break up for half term and I was sorting out activities for the following week. Bloody hell, that means I'm possibly fifteen weeks pregnant. How can that be?'

'You need to do a test.' That would be the first thing October would do, if she found herself in the same situation. 'Then if you definitely are pregnant, you should make an appointment with your doctor.'

Petra screwed up her eyes. 'I know. I'll buy one later. I was awake most of last night worrying about it. What if I'm not pregnant and it's something else?'

'Like what?'

Petra stared at her, her face bleak.

October shook her head. 'Now you're being daft.' She wanted to give her a hug, but she didn't dare. Her boss didn't come across as the hugging type. 'You're pregnant,' she stated firmly. 'And the sooner you do a test and put your mind at rest the better.'

Petra didn't look convinced, and October got the distinct impression that she wasn't thrilled about her impending motherhood.

'Keep this to yourself, eh? Please?' Petra asked.

'Of course I will. You can trust me not to say anything,' October promised.

Picklewick's high street was usually busy, and today was no exception. After the conversation with October, Petra decided to strike while the iron was hot and pop into the village to buy a test, but when she saw the number of people waiting to be served in the chemist, she bottled it.

Besides, the staff there knew her. Ditto the tiny supermarket. Petra didn't want to risk being seen, or risk someone idly mentioning to Amos that they'd seen her browsing the aisles for a pregnancy test.

If she **was** pregnant, it was only right that Harry should be the first to know. Besides, she wanted to break the news to Amos herself.

She felt sick when she thought of telling them. Maybe if she knew how Harry would react, she could at least brace herself. Amos, she was sure, would be very disappointed in her.

The nearest big supermarket was nine miles away, but at least her anonymity would be guaranteed. There would only be a small chance of her bumping into anyone she knew; she could put twenty tests in her basket and no one would bat an eyelid.

Even so, Petra parked the car at the furthest end of the car park and slunk inside. She grabbed a basket, and on her way to the correct aisle she threw a couple of things into it because she didn't want anyone to think she'd come in for the sole purpose of buying a pregnancy test.

Feeling very self-conscious and a little ridiculous, Petra found the shelf she was looking for and hastily glanced around to check that no one was watching.

No one was, so she moved closer and studied the various boxes.

Flippin' heck, who knew there would be so many to choose from? Did they all do different things? Were the more expensive ones more reliable than the cheaper ones?

Not wanting to ask, Petra grabbed a couple of mid-range ones and dropped them on top of the packet of salad leaves and the half a quiche she'd already put in there, and hurried to the checkout, wondering why on earth she'd shoved the quiche in. She didn't even particularly **like** quiche. Not daring to put it back in the chiller she'd got it from, she joined the queue at the self-service checkout and waited impatiently for a free till.

'Hiya, fancy seeing you here.'

Petra jumped guiltily as she recognised the voice, and her heart plummeted.

Cher Reynolds, who had made a play for Harry when he'd first moved to Picklewick, was standing behind her in the queue.

Petra rolled her eyes – that was just what she needed. **Not.**

Feeling scruffy in her jodhpurs and old riding boots, Petra tried not to look at Cher's glossy shoulder-length hair, long nails, expertly made-up face and immaculately trendy clothes.

Then she realised Cher was examining her basket and Petra hurriedly pulled the bag of salad leaves over the top of the pregnancy tests. Hopefully the damned woman hadn't seen them.

'How are you keeping?' Cher asked, her eyes still on the contents of Petra's basket.

'Great. You?'

'Thalia is doing brilliantly at her new stables. They're simply wonderful with her.'

'Good, glad to hear it.'

'How's business?'

'Fine.' Just at that moment a till became free and with a tight smile, Petra scurried over to it.

'Bye,' Cher called after her, but Petra ignored her. She'd never liked the woman and didn't see the point in making small talk with her. Hopefully another six months would pass before she would set eyes on her again.

All thoughts of Cher were cast out of Petra's mind as she drove home, and were replaced by a steady worry about what the two boxes in her bag would tell her.

She'd do both the tests, just in case. Perhaps she should have bought another one, then she could have had the best out of three, but even as she was thinking it, she knew a false result was unlikely. Both tests would either be positive or negative.

Please be negative, she prayed sometime later in the privacy of the bathroom, after peeing on both of the plastic sticks. But deep down she knew they wouldn't be, and when a second line appeared in the little window, her fears were confirmed.

Petra was unquestionably pregnant.

Harry, I'm pregnant. No, that was too blunt. Petra gathered up the evidence, and as she went outside to pop it in the wheelie bin, she tried another approach.

Harry, you're going to be a father.

Maybe she should start with that? She might finish with it too, if Harry walked out in shock and refused to speak to her again.

That was the issue – Petra was terrified it would spoil things between them. It was going to change everything, regardless of whether he was happy about it or not. Nothing would be the same again, and she didn't think she was ready for that.

She'd tell him tomorrow; which would allow her to indulge in one more afternoon and evening of normality, one more day of his love, because once he knew there was no going back.

There was no hurry to tell him just yet. One more day wouldn't hurt, and it would give her a chance to work out how she was going to cope. She was barely holding things together financially as it was, and that was with her often working fifteen-hour days, even with October's help. Owning horses was hard work. Running your own business was hard work. Put the two together...

Harry's idea of turning the cowshed into cottages was a lovely one, but a pie-in-the-sky one. Especially now, if he ran screaming for the hills when she told him about the baby. Even if he was willing to stand by her, she would have too much on her plate with the impending new arrival to even consider adding another problem. And whilst the income from the cottages might make the difference between the stables staying afloat or going under, she couldn't afford the initial outlay.

What a mess. How could she bring a baby into this?

But that was the issue, wasn't it, because she had every intention of bringing a baby into it. She might still be in shock and she had no idea which way was up, she mightn't have considered a child to be part of her life or never had any wish to be a mother – but she **was** having one and suddenly Petra felt intensely protective of the little scrap growing inside her.

Didn't that man ever give up, October asked herself as she saw another message from Zeus on her phone.

We need to talk, it said.

The hell we do, she thought. He had nothing to say to her that she could possibly want to hear, and he definitely wouldn't like what she had to say to him if ever the two of them met again. Which was unlikely. Zeus and October lived in very different worlds now, and she didn't envy him his one little bit. She was perfectly happy in her own.

She couldn't think what he wanted to talk about, unless his new beau had also dumped him. Zeus was a man who didn't like being without female company for long, so she wouldn't put it past him to expect that if he clicked his fingers October would come running.

 She would bet her last penny that he'd assume he would be able to sweet talk her back into his bed.

Hoping to prevent Zeus from contacting her again, she sent a reply back – **We have nothing to talk about** – then she blocked his number.

That would put an end to his shenanigans, and October couldn't think why she hadn't blocked him before now.

One thing was certain though: even if she had been tempted to return to Zeus's yard, October couldn't leave a pregnant woman in the lurch. Whether Petra liked it or not, a baby was going to turn her life upside down, starting from today. The woman was going to need all the help she could get.

And there was also another reason: an even more compelling one.

Luca.

Harry paused and glanced up and down the street before he stepped into the jewellers on the way home from his last client of the day. He was fairly certain Petra was safely at the stables, but he wasn't taking any chances. He wanted his proposal to be a complete surprise and he was determined that she wasn't going to get wind of what he was planning.

'Are you able to resize this?' he asked, taking the ring out of his pocket, unwrapping the tissue he'd folded it up in, and handing it to the lady behind the counter.

She picked it up and turned it over, studying it. 'Eighteen-carat gold. Is it to be made larger or smaller?'

'Smaller, please.' In order to discover whether the ring fitted her, Harry had boxed clever – so he'd thought – and had waited until Petra was soundly asleep last night, and had then carefully slipped the ring onto her finger without waking her.

It had taken a while for her to drop off to sleep, which was surprising considering how exhausted she'd looked. She'd had dark circles around her eyes and had hardly touched the evening meal Amos had cooked. Putting everything together, Harry wondered if she was more worried about the stables' finances than she was letting on. Something was on her mind, because she'd been withdrawn and preoccupied all evening. Maybe he shouldn't have mentioned his idea of converting the cowshed into holiday lets – it was one more worry she didn't need.

Anyway, after Valentine's Day, she wouldn't need to worry any more. What was his would be hers, and the money in his bank account should be enough to cover the renovations, with some left over.

After explaining to the sales assistant what he'd done and being informed that slipping a ring on someone's finger and seeing how loose it was wasn't an accurate gauge for resizing, he also explained that he'd need it back by the 12th February at the latest. It was cutting it fine, but when Harry told the jeweller what he was planning, she took pity on him and assured him it would be ready in time.

Right, he thought, stepping outside, all he needed to do now was to book a table somewhere special, which might be easier said than done; all the best places were probably fully booked for Valentine's Day. But maybe Amos could recommend somewhere?

Before Harry walked back to his car, he gave Amos a call.

'You'll be lucky,' Amos said when Harry asked him. 'Anywhere decent will cost a fortune – it's like the florists, they hike the prices up just because they can. Why don't you eat here?'

'At the stables?' He turned his back on the street and stared at the engagement rings in the window. They all looked the same. The one which had belonged to Amos's wife was striking and unique, and he couldn't wait to see it on Petra's finger.

'Why not?' Amos asked. 'It's the place she loves the best. Don't worry, I'll make myself scarce. Oh, and don't bother with all that nonsense of putting the ring in the bottom of a champagne glass or burying it in a trifle – she won't thank you for it.'

Harry thought about Amos's suggestion. Petra probably wouldn't want to have dinner in a fancy restaurant, so Amos had a point. Anyway, she might suspect something was up if he suggested going out, and he wanted it to be a complete surprise.

'Good idea,' he said to Amos. 'It's going to be tricky keeping it from her, though.'

'We'll think of something.'

'Okay, let's do it. I just hope she says yes.'

'Why wouldn't she? She loves the bones of you, and you feel the same way about her.'

Harry did, at that. Petra was the best thing that had ever happened to him.

He was grinning madly to himself and was about to walk away, when a figure blocked his path.

'Hello, stranger.'

Harry stifled a sigh. The last person he wanted to see was Cher Reynolds. He hadn't forgiven her for being bitchy about Petra when he'd first moved to Picklewick.

'Hi, Cher,' he replied, with a distinct lack of enthusiasm.

'I haven't seen you or Petra for ages, then I bump into both of you on the same day.' Cher gave him a knowing look and smirked. 'I saw Petra in the supermarket earlier. I was surprised to see her, to be honest – I didn't think grocery shopping was her thing.'

Neither did Harry and he briefly wondered what she'd been doing there. Cher seemed to be waiting for a reply, but all he did was shrug, hoping she'd take the hint and go away.

She continued to stare at him and, feeling uncomfortable under her scrutiny, he was about to make his excuses and hurry off, when she said, 'Am I allowed to congratulate you?'

Trust her to jump to the right conclusion. He shouldn't have lingered outside the jewellers.

'Um...' He hesitated, wondering if it was a good idea to ask her not to say anything in case she bumped into Petra again, or whether him mentioning it would only make her want to gossip to every man, woman and child in the village, just to spite him.

Cher gazed at the display of engagement rings in the window, her expression thoughtful, then she looked at him and smiled. 'I'm sorry, have I jumped the gun?'

'A bit.' He didn't want to say much more.'

'I take it the wedding will be before the baby arrives?'

Harry stared blankly back at her. He had no clue what she was talking about. 'I'm sorry...?'

 Cher smirked at him. 'She hasn't told, you, has she?'

'Told me what?'

'Petra was buying a pregnancy test when I saw her earlier.' Cher leaned closer. 'I must say, she has put on a bit of weight around her middle already.' She placed a hand on his arm. 'You must make sure she isn't still riding when she's eight months pregnant.'

Harry was frozen to the spot. 'Pregnant,' he repeated, and as he said it, everything fell into place and he knew without a doubt that what Cher said was true. **Petra was pregnant**.

The signs had all been there if only he'd looked, and he wondered how long she'd known. Not long, he surmised. Why hadn't she mentioned the possibility to him? Then he thought that maybe she didn't want to get his hopes up until she was certain.

They hadn't discussed having children, but he'd always hoped he'd be a father one day—

'Are you all right?' Cher asked.

'Fine. Never better,' he said, absently.

He couldn't wait to get home, he was so excited. But he'd hang fire until she brought the subject up. She'd probably wait until they were alone anyway – it was unlikely she'd announce it over the dinner table with Amos there, although Harry knew Petra's uncle would be just as thrilled at the news as Harry. Of course, there was always the possibility that it might be a false alarm...

But if Petra **was** pregnant, Harry would be more than thrilled – he'd be **overjoyed**.

'I'm sorry,' October whispered in Luca's ear. 'My mum insisted. She's been going on so much about meeting you, that I agreed in order to shut her up. I hope you don't mind?'

October looked anxious, but Luca didn't mind in the slightest. In fact, he was delighted to think that October had told her mother about him. It made their relationship seem all the more real and solid. He decided he'd take her to meet his parents before too long: they would be delighted.

Lena was an older version of October, with the same shaped eyes and mouth, and the same dark hair, although Lena's sported considerably more grey.

'Hello, I'm October's mum. I'm so glad she's met someone nice.'

'Mum!' October looked mortified and hissed, 'Stop talking. Please!'

Luca barked out a laugh – this must be where October got her forthright way of speaking from. 'Pleased to meet you,' he said.

Lena simpered. 'I don't get to meet any of her friends very often because she always moves around so much. It does worry me, you know, October going from yard to yard. Something went on at the last place she was at, but she won't tell me what. Perhaps she's told you?'

'Sorry, Mum, we've got to go or we'll be late.' October, who was blushing furiously, grabbed his arm and pulled him down the path.

Lena called after them, 'Will you be home later? Or—'

'Gotta run! Bye!' October scampered towards the car, dragging Luca who was chortling like mad.

Her mother was hilarious, he thought, although October didn't appear to think so.

'I'm so sorry,' October began, but Luca stopped her with a kiss.

'It's fine,' he said. No doubt his parents would be just as embarrassing. It didn't matter how old you were, parents always had the ability to reduce you to an awkward teen.

It was only later when he and October were lying in his bed, October asleep on his chest, that Luca had time to muse on what her mother had said about October moving from yard to yard.

October had definitely come to Picklewick under a cloud, and although she had shared the reason with him he wondered whether she truly intended to remain here working at a small riding school, when she'd travelled the world as a groom. She was used to far more excitement than either this village or Luca could offer her.

Would she be content to live here, or would she get itchy feet and want to leave?

Luca prayed he'd be enough of a reason for her to stay, but he had an awful feeling that he might not be.

CHAPTER SEVEN

Petra hadn't said a word last night. Not one single word. Harry had waited on tenterhooks, for her to tell him her news, but nothing, so he'd come to the conclusion that there **was** no news. No pregnancy, no baby, no impending fatherhood.

He had been awake half the night, feeling upset. Which was ridiculous – fancy lamenting the loss of something you never had in the first place?

But this morning everything changed.

Normally Harry would be long gone by eight o'clock, on his way to his first shoeing of the day. But his van was in the garage for an MOT and a service, and without a vehicle he couldn't work, so he was hanging around the stables trying to make himself useful until his van was ready to collect. He'd considered waiting at the garage, hoping his lurking presence would hurry them along, but common sense prevailed and he'd asked Amos to follow behind him in the Land Rover when he dropped the van off. Amos had then brought him back to the stables for a couple of hours where he could at least be of some use. Timothy was due this morning to give the horses their annual booster shots, so he guessed that an extra pair of hands would come in useful.

Last night Harry had forgotten to put the bins at the top of the lane ready for collection, so the first thing he did when he got out of the Land Rover was to drag them to where they needed to be. There were two wheelie bins, one for general waste and one for all manner of recyclable items. But as he manoeuvred the general waste bin, it caught on the side of the fence and to his dismay toppled onto its side

The lid flew open and a disgustingly large amount of rubbish fell out. Thankfully most of it was in plastic bags so at least he didn't have to pick up loose stuff with his bare hands.

There was one thing he had to pick up though, and that was a small white plastic stick. It was about as long as his forefinger and had a bulbous bit on one end with two lines on it.

He immediately guessed what it was, and he stared at it curiously.

It was a pregnancy test.

Sadness pricked at him and as he bent down to retrieve it, he noticed that the cardboard box it came in and the instruction leaflet were lying on the ground next to it.

Tutting because those two things should have been placed into the recycling bin and not the general waste, he picked them up, but as he did so his eyes scanned across part of the leaflet.

It was the part which said **"one line, not pregnant, two lines, pregnant."**

He carefully looked at the pee stick. Then he read the instructions again.

What the—?

Petra was **pregnant**?

He didn't know whether to leap for joy or thump the nearest fence post.

He was thrilled, delighted, awed, and several other wonderful emotions: but he was also dismayed and upset that she hadn't told him.

Harry took a steadying breath and let it out slowly. Maybe she needed a few days to come to terms with it first? He knew he was going to take a while for the news to sink in, so he empathised with her. She'd tell him when she was ready. He didn't know how he was going to keep a lid on his excitement until then, though.

Putting the evidence into the correct bins, he cleared up the rest of the mess, wheeled them into position and went to find Petra. Even if he had to keep his mouth shut for the time being, at least he could give her a cuddle.

October found she was humming to herself a lot lately. On the short drive to work she always listened to the radio and often a song would get stuck in her head and play on repeat and she'd end up singing it all day. It usually irritated her, but since she'd been dating Luca, she quite enjoyed it. The animals didn't seem to mind either, and she had the impression the hens positively liked it.

They were laying brilliantly, and over the past few days she'd taken it upon herself to release them from their coop in the mornings, then root around in the warm straw for the eggs. It was a soothing and pleasant interlude between taking the horses and ponies to the fields and starting the other jobs that needed doing. She hadn't yet turned the horses out this morning though, because the vet, Timothy, was due to arrive to give them their annual vaccinations so they were still in their stalls. She'd be on hand if she was needed, but Petra would be overseeing the process, so she strolled off to see to the chickens.

Thinking of Petra, October wondered how she was feeling. She hadn't spoken to her since their conversation yesterday, although she knew that Petra had popped out for the sole purpose of buying a pregnancy test. October was convinced it would be positive.

Smiling, she pushed aside a broody hen and felt underneath her for the egg, the bird's feathers tickling her hand.

'Thank you, Rita,' she said. The hen looked at her out of one beady eye.

October added it to the others in the basket and straightened up. She'd take these to the kitchen before beginning the mucking out. Forking up soiled straw wasn't a task she particularly liked, but when you owned or worked with horses it was a fact of life.

At least it was good exercise, and along with riding it kept her reasonably fit, so she was looking forward to a ride later on. Petra had told her she could have all the rides she wanted, fitting them in during her free time. She'd probably go out later, before the lessons started, and maybe Luca would come with her. Him being his own boss had its advantages, and being able to come and go as he pleased was one of them.

Hearing a vehicle on the lane as she walked across the yard to the house, October looked around, expecting it to be Timothy. But when she saw the flash four-by-four, she immediately recognised it and its personalized number plate: ZEUS 1.

What the hell was he doing here?

She waited for the car to come to a halt (in the middle of the yard, for goodness' sake!), her heart in her mouth, tension making her head pound. A small muscle beneath her left eye began to twitch and she blinked furiously.

Zeus slowly emerged from the driver's seat, took his sunglasses off (what a pratt – it wasn't even sunny), leaned against the car door and stared at her, his head tilted to the side. 'Please don't cry. You know I can't cope with crying.'

October stopped blinking and opened her eyes wide, overcompensating. 'I'm **not** crying. What do you want?'

'To talk. Is there somewhere we could go? I'd suggest we go for a drive, but…' He trailed off and glanced meaningfully at her boots. They were covered in manure and mud.

For a man who lived and breathed horses, Zeus was oddly reluctant to deal with the mucky side of equine ownership.

October hesitated. Seeing him standing there in all his handsome self-assurance, like a model out of Horse and Hound (minus the horses and the hounds), threw her off-kilter. He was still devilishly handsome and very charismatic, but he no longer made her insides flip or her heart flutter. In fact, apart from the obvious – good looks, fame and wealth – she didn't know what she'd seen in him.

However, she **was** curious. Now that he was here, it wouldn't hurt to hear him out and then she could send him away with a flea in his ear. Anyway, this couldn't take long because she needed to get on with the mucking out or she'd have Petra on her case.

'Please,' he said, plastering a winning smile on his face. He often used it to get his own way, and it usually worked. He was good at turning on the charm.

The feed store would be empty at this time of day, so with a quick glance around the yard, she said, 'This way,' and marched off.

She heard the car door click shut and his firm footsteps behind her as she led the way.

He followed her inside, his gaze scanning the tubs of grains and the buckets stacked to one side and came to rest on a handwritten list pinned to the wall. 'What are you doing in a place like this, Toby?'

Toby? Grrr. Once upon a time she used to love his nickname for her. Now it only served to set her teeth on edge. 'Working,' she snapped. She put the basket of eggs carefully down on the ground and folded her arms.

'You are better than this.' He waved an arm dismissively.

'I needed a job.'

'Yes, but...' He shuddered.

'You sacked me, remember? I took what I could get.'

'I "let you go" – there's a difference. And I had no choice, you know that.'

If he was here to persuade her to go back to him, he was doing a poor job of it. He could at least have brought her flowers or begged her forgiveness. All he'd succeeded in doing was dissing her job and making her cross.

'What do you want? Why are you even here?' she asked with a sigh.

'I need a favour, and you've blocked my number so...' He held out his hands in a what-else-do-you-expect-me-to-do gesture.

'A favour? That's rich considering what you did.'

'I wouldn't ask, but I'm desperate. I need you to tell Minnow a small fib. I could make it worth your while?'

'If you think I'm coming back to you or your yard, you've got a nerve.'

'I think we both know that's not going to happen, don't we? We've moved on since then.'

'Yeah, you certainly have,' she said, thinking of him with another woman only days after he'd "let **her** go".

'Don't be petty. We'd had our fun, but we'd run our course.'

'So you thought you'd run another one with someone else?'

'It was only a quick kiss. It didn't mean anything.'

'Yeah, right. And Minnow believes that, does she?' October saw the expression on Zeus's face and said slowly, 'You haven't told her that it wasn't me in that photo, have you? Do you realise she phoned my boss because she thought you were still seeing me? You need to tell her the truth.'

'That's the problem – I told her it **was** you.'

'Why would you do something like that?' October cried. 'What's wrong with you?'

'I had to. If she knew I was seeing someone else, Minnow would have left me for good.'

'I was under the impression she'd left you anyway? She mentioned something to my boss about you living on fresh air?'

'That's why I need a favour from you. I wouldn't ask if I wasn't desperate.'

'What's the favour?'

'I want you to tell Minnow that it **was** you in the photo, and that when it was taken you'd thrown yourself at me and you were begging me to take you back. She'd believe you. Especially if you said I didn't want anything to do with you.'

October couldn't believe what she was hearing. This was surreal. He'd lied to her, slept with her, then sacked her, and now he wanted her to take the blame?

Hardly!

Zeus stepped closer and took hold of her hands, a pleading look on his face. 'Please, please, please. For the sake of my marriage. You must call her and tell her it was all your fault, that I didn't know you were going to be there, that you were causing a scene and begging me to take you back, and that I was trying to get away from you. Please?'

October was about to tell him where to go, when something outside the door caught her eye.

Luca was standing less than ten feet away. His expression was tight, his mouth a thin line.

Dragging her hands free of Zeus's grasp, she hurried towards him, but before she'd taken more than two steps he turned smartly on his heel and strode off.

'Toby, wait!' Zeus grabbed her sleeve and hauled her back.

'Let go of me,' she snarled.

'Not until you say you'll help. Please, Toby, you don't know what's at stake.'

'Oh, I'm pretty certain I do. Now let go of me, before I scream.'

Zeus released her, and October shot out of the door and hared across the yard.

But she was too late.

The last glimpse she saw of the man she was falling in love with was the tail lights of his Range Rover as he sped down the lane.

'What are you doing?' Harry demanded, incredulously, striding up to the loosebox Petra was working in.

'What does it look like?' she retorted in a clipped voice. 'I'm mucking out.' She was carrying bales of straw into the stall and she looked as grumpy as hell.

Well, so was he, after seeing this. Actually, grumpy didn't cover it – he was furious. Those bales were darned heavy, and she was **pregnant**, for god's sake!

'Do you honestly think that's a good idea?' he demanded.

'I always muck out.'

'I don't care. October should be doing that – where is she, anyway? You shouldn't be lifting bales of sodding straw in your condition.'

He watched her pause as what he'd said sunk in.

She had her back to him, and she stiffened. Without turning around, she said in a small voice, 'What condition is that?'

'Don't play games, Petra. I **know**, okay? You've got to think of the baby.'

Suddenly she sparked into life and whirled around to face him. 'What do you **think** I've been thinking about?'

Harry stabbed a finger at the bales of straw. 'Clearly not our child!'

'How dare you!' She stormed towards him and for a moment he thought she was going to deck him, but she barged on past and he quickly stepped to the side.

'Wait...Petra, let's talk.'

'I'm going to talk, all right,' she yelled over her shoulder. 'Some people need to learn to keep their mouths shut.'

And with that she was gone, leaving Harry stunned.

He debated whether he should go after her, but Petra had a temper and it wasn't a wise idea to try to apologise when she was so angry. He'd give it an hour. Hopefully, she'd have calmed down by then.

Needing to work off his own ire, he did the only thing he could think of – he carried on where she'd left off and mucked out the sodding stall.

October stood in the yard staring after Luca and wishing she'd never set eyes on Zeus Fernsby. The man was a menace. She heaved a sigh and blew out her cheeks. She wasn't sure how much or what portion of the conversation Luca had heard, but he'd listened to enough of it to get the wrong end of the stick.

Oh god, and here was Petra with a bee in her bonnet. She had a face like thunder and she was peed off about something – probably because October was late doing the mucking out. This morning wasn't turning out to be one of her better days.

'Toby?' Zeus asked.

Huh? Was he still here? 'Get lost.'

'Who the hell is this and what's he doing in my yard?' Petra demanded, marching up to them.

'He's no one and he's just leaving.' October glared at him, daring Zeus to contradict her.

Zeus spluttered, 'But—'

'Sod off.' October scowled menacingly.

Seeing he wasn't going to get anywhere, Zeus shook his head sadly, and sauntered towards his car.

Thank goodness he was leaving without a fuss, October thought, but when he reached his car, he paused and smiled at her. It was the sort of smile a hyena might give to an antelope just before he ate it for lunch. 'You'd better hang on to this measly little job,' he said, 'because I'll make sure you never work in a decent yard again. Your name will be mud. Ciao, Toby.'

October poked her tongue out at him. It was more likely to be the other way around by the time Minnow finished with him. He might have the talent, but it was his wife's money that paid for his fabulous horses and their hideously expensive upkeep.

Pulling herself together and knowing there was nothing she could do about Luca right now – she'd speak to him later, and explain – she said to Petra, 'I'll just take the eggs in to Amos, then I'll get on with the mucking out.'

When she saw Petra's expression, her heart sank.

'What have you got to say for yourself?' Petra demanded.

'I'm sorry...?' October was confused. What was she supposed to have done? If it was about Zeus, she hadn't asked him to come to the stables and he'd gone now, so—

'You **told** him.' Petra had her hands on her hips and murder in her eyes.

'Told who what?'

'Harry?'

'What am I supposed to have—? Oh...'

'Well?'

'I didn't tell him anything. Does that mean you're definitely pregnant?'

'It's none of your business whether I am or not. I don't appreciate you gossiping about me. I don't care who it is. You don't go running to Harry after I expressly told you not to.'

As far as October could recall, Petra hadn't issued a direct order – she'd asked. But even if she hadn't, October wouldn't have dreamt of saying anything to anyone.

'I didn't,' she repeated.

'**Someone** did and the only person who knew was **you**.'

'It wasn't me!'

Petra glowered at her and shook her head. 'I'm not going to argue with you. Harry knows, and someone told him. It can only be you.'

Sod this; October had enough. She'd thought she was settling in at the stables on Muddypuddle Lane and that Petra was starting to view her as a friend and not just as an employee.

Obviously not.

The woman had leapt in, throwing accusations around, and was refusing to listen to her protestations of innocence.

'I resign,' October said, slowly and distinctly.

'You what?'

'I resign. I don't like being accused of something I haven't done, so you can stick your job. I'm out of here.'

And with that, she did just as Zeus had done minutes earlier – she left the stables on Muddypuddle Lane. But unlike Zeus, she was trying not to cry.

Where else was she going to get a job working with horses within easy travelling distance of her mum's house?

Hopefully, when she explained why Zeus had been at the stables, her relationship with Luca would be back on an even keel, because she didn't think she could take any more upsets today.

Luca's heart was pounding as he drove down the lane, faster than was wise. He couldn't believe what he'd just heard. That poor man.

He was finding it difficult to reconcile the woman he thought he knew with the woman that Zeus Fernsby had been pleading with. Begging, even. The poor man's marriage was on the rocks and October was still chasing him, not caring who she hurt.

It was despicable that she'd do something like that. He thought she was different, but she wasn't.

Luca shook his head in disgust. She'd been stringing him along, probably using him as a back-up in case she didn't get back together with Zeus. Zeus was the better prospect – Luca was the reserve. What a—!

He was tempted to call her all the names under the sun, but instead he pulled into the side of the road, reached for his phone and blocked her number. Just in time, because she'd already sent him a message which he deleted without reading.

It was going to be difficult stabling Midnight at Petra's place with October around, but he had a feeling she wouldn't be there for long. As much as he was tempted to move his horse to another yard, he decided to hang on for a while. He liked the stables on Muddypuddle Lane, damn it, and it was convenient too. Why should he have to move Midnight, when October was the one at fault?

He'd simply have to do his best to avoid her and wait for her to find some other mug to latch on to.

But even as those thoughts were travelling through his mind, along with the anger and the hurt he was feeling he also felt a stab of pain and an ache in his heart. He could so easily have fallen in love with her.

An incredible loneliness and feeling of loss swept over him, and for the first time in years, Luca felt like crying.

CHAPTER EIGHT

Harry dusted stray stalks of dried grass off his clothes and stood back. He'd mucked out the stall and as he was doing so he'd used the time to practice what he was going to say to Petra when he caught up with her. He knew she might still be mad, but they had to talk. Not just for their own sakes, but for the baby.

He still couldn't believe he was going to be a father. Wow. It was mind-blowing and he was as scared as hell. What if he was a hopeless dad? He might be awful at it. But even if he was, he knew one thing – he'd love it with every cell in his body. He already did. The thought that Petra had his baby growing inside her, made his heart melt.

He wondered how far gone she was. Had she seen a doctor yet? Probably not, if she'd only just found out. What about scans? Would he be allowed to go with her? He wanted to be as involved as humanly possible, to be as supportive as possible.

But first, he needed to find her and apologise.

She was finishing up with Timothy, handing over the lead ropes of the last two ponies for Nathan to take to the field, when Harry veered towards Nathan, and said quietly, 'Can you finish off the mucking out? I need to speak to Petra and I haven't clapped eyes on October this morning.'

'You won't, neither,' Nathan said. 'She quit.'

'Why? I thought she was getting on okay.'

'Petra didn't say why, but I think they've had a bust-up. I'd keep out of her way if I were you – she's got a face like a slapped arse.'

'Erm, that might be my fault.' Harry winced. 'I'll tell you about it later.' He clapped Nathan on the shoulder and walked over to his brother. 'Timothy, are you all done?'

'Yep. That's it for another year.' Timothy picked up a box and tucked it under his arm. 'See you, Petra.'

Petra gave Timothy a tight smile. She didn't even look at Harry.

Harry waited for his brother to move out of earshot before saying, 'I'm sorry. It took me by surprise that's all, and when I saw you humping blimmin' great bales around, I lost it for a minute.'

She sighed and finally looked him in the eye. 'I should have told you. It wasn't fair you having to hear it from someone else.'

'Cher said she'd seen you in the supermarket. I had, erm, popped into Picklewick to pick up, erm, um, never mind. And I bumped into her. She couldn't wait to tell me.'

Her eyes widened. '**Cher Reynolds** told you I was pregnant?'

'Yeah, why? Who did you think it was? Who else knows?'

Petra hung her head. 'Rose Walker guessed, and so did October. Honestly, the idea hadn't entered my head before then, so I thought I'd better buy a test. I did it yesterday afternoon. It was positive.'

'I know. I saw it in the bin.'

She looked up at him from under her lashes, and her eyes glistened with tears. 'I'm sorry. I just didn't know how to tell you.' She let out a sob and Harry groaned.

Gathering her into his arms, he said, 'It's okay, no harm done. I know now, and that's all that matters. There's no need to get so upset.' He kissed the top of her head and held her tighter.

'Aren't you annoyed?'

'About Cher telling me? It couldn't be helped. But I was annoyed when I saw you mucking out the stable. You've got to look after yourself.'

'I meant, are you annoyed about me getting pregnant?'

Harry drew back to look at her face. 'I don't understand. Why should I be annoyed about that? I'm absolutely delighted. Did you honestly think I'd be mad?'

Petra sniffed. 'Yes.'

'Is that the reason you didn't tell me straight away?'

'Yes.'

'What made you believe I wouldn't want this baby?' He was thoroughly bemused.

'We've never talked about having kids. I didn't think you'd want children after looking after Timothy for all those years.'

'I did what I had to do as far as Timothy was concerned, and I don't begrudge him a second of it. But Timothy is my brother, not my son. I **want** this baby, Petra. I want to be a father. And I want **you**.'

'But how am I going to manage?' she wailed.

'Don't you mean how are **we** going to manage? I'm part of this, too, you know.' He grinned down at her. 'What exactly are you fretting about?'

'The stables, duh.' She gave him a tiny, worried smile.

'We'll be fine. People get pregnant and have babies every day, and they cope.'

'I won't be able to do half of what I did before. And when the baby comes, I'll be spending most of my time looking after it!'

'It'll be okay. We'll work something out.'

'October resigned.' Petra screwed her eyes shut and took a deep breath before opening them again.

'Nathan told me. Do you know why?'

'It's my fault. I accused her of telling you I was expecting. I'm such an idiot. I should never have flown off the handle.'

Harry agreed that she shouldn't have, but he thought it best not to say anything. He kissed the tip of her nose instead.

'I'd better apologise,' she added. 'And not just because we need her, but because it's the right thing to do.'

October threw her phone down on the coffee table and slumped back onto the sofa. Either Luca had turned his mobile off or he'd blocked her. She strongly suspected the latter because none of the messages she'd sent him had been delivered.

Once again, her eyes filled with tears and she brushed them away angrily. She wouldn't cry. **She wouldn't.**

If he chose not to give her a chance to explain, that was his loss.

She rubbed her eyes with her knuckles and gritted her teeth. It had been a pretty awful day all round. Not only had she lost her job, but she appeared to have lost her boyfriend too. She might not have been working at the stables on Muddypuddle Lane for long, but she'd liked it – and she might have only known Luca for a short amount of time, but she was starting to fall for him. Early days or not, she'd begun to harbour a tiny hope that he might be The One.

How silly of her!

He'd baled on her at the first hurdle, which made her wish she'd never taken him up on his challenge when he'd come a cropper the day he'd been showing off over the jumps. If she'd walked away then, she wouldn't be in the mess she was in now.

Thinking that she ought to start looking for another job so at least she'd be able to tell her mum she'd applied for something, she eyed her phone balefully.

The way she felt at the moment, she'd apply for anything as long as it was a couple of hundred miles away from Picklewick. Or Kent. She had no desire to go back there, either.

Suddenly she remembered something Zeus had said, and it made her sit up and groan. Hadn't he threatened to sully her name and make sure she was persona non grata in showjumping circles? Damn it, he had.

He couldn't possibly inform every single yard in the country, but gossip was rife in the horsey community and he was incredibly well known, so news would travel fast, especially since he'd be putting it about that October had ruined his marriage. He'd do anything to salvage it – it was just a pity he hadn't considered how much he'd stood to lose **before** he'd taken October to bed.

If he could have an affair with her and then leap straight into another with this unknown woman in the photo, the odds were that he had slept with other women in the past and had got away with it, so he'd probably assumed he would get away with it this time.

October had been incredibly blind not to have realised what he was like.

She still couldn't believe the cheek of him driving halfway across the country to try to talk her into helping him out of the pickle he'd got himself in. His arrogance had cost her her job at the stables on Muddypuddle Lane and her relationship with a man who she'd been starting to fall for.

Oh, who was she kidding? She **had** fallen for him. Hard.

The sound of the doorbell ringing roused her from her pity party for a second as she debated whether to bother answering it. She was about to sink back into misery, when a thought occurred to her and she scrambled to her feet and hurried into the hall.

'Oh, it's you,' she said, on opening the door and seeing Petra standing on the step. 'What do you want?'

'To apologise.'

'Hmph.'

'I shouldn't have jumped to conclusions.'

'Damned right, you shouldn't have.'

'Can I come in? Or is your mum home, because if she is, I don't want to intrude.'

'She's at work.' October opened the door wider and stood to the side. 'Congratulations?'

A smile lit Petra's face as she nodded.

'I'm happy for you,' October said, coming to a halt in the middle of the living room and crossing her arms.

'I'm happy for me, too. I think.' Petra hesitated, the sudden silence acute, then she said, 'Would you consider coming back to work at the stables? Please? Will it help if I blame it on the hormones?' She made a wry face. 'Scrap that – I'm just a sour cow with a quick temper. I really am sorry.'

She did indeed look sorry, October thought. Although Petra was in a steady relationship with a great guy, October had seen for herself how scared she'd been about telling Harry, so she said, 'Apology accepted.'

'Thank you. Will you come back?'

'Um...' October paused, thinking furiously. 'I don't think so.'

Petra's face fell. 'I promise nothing like this will ever happen again.'

'Luca and I have split up.'

'Oh, dear. Was it anything to do with the guy who was at the stables earlier?'

'Zeus. Yes. Remember that photo I showed you of him and the woman with long hair? Luca overheard a conversation where Zeus was trying to persuade me to tell Minnow it was me in the photo and that I had been begging him to take me back.'

'Pft! If his wife believes that, she must be stupid. He had his hand on the woman's backside, for a start.'

'I know, but he's desperate – she's the one with the money.'

'Can't you go to Luca and explain?'

'He's not taking my calls. I'm pretty sure he's blocked me.'

'Give him time – he'll come round.'

'I don't care if he does or doesn't. I don't want him in my life if he reacts like that at the slightest misunderstanding. I'm done with him. I'm done with men, full stop. I've had enough work-related romances to last me a lifetime. It leads to nothing but awkwardness at best, and an untenable working environment at worst.'

'That shouldn't stop you from coming back to the stables.'

Bless her, Petra looked so hopeful, that October nearly changed her mind. However, she knew she'd regret it if she did. 'I can't face seeing him,' she admitted.

Petra gazed at her quizzically and October squirmed under the woman's scrutiny. 'You really like him, don't you?'

'And that's the problem.'

'I can fix that – I'll tell him to take Midnight elsewhere.'

The generous offer almost made October cry. 'You can't do that. You need his livery fees to pay me. You said so yourself.'

Petra sank into the nearest chair, and October felt awful for not inviting a pregnant woman to sit down. 'What will you do?' Petra asked.

October sat opposite her. 'I honestly don't know.'

'Would you say I'm a meddler?' Petra asked Harry later that afternoon. Harry had just arrived home and Petra had been itching to talk to him. Since she'd returned from October's house, she'd been thinking, and a plan had begun to form. But if she decided to act on it, she wanted to make sure Harry was on board. She also had a suspicion she might be interfering in something that wasn't her business.

On the other hand, she'd seen the way October and Luca looked at each other, and there was definitely a great deal of emotion and passion. It seemed a shame to waste it.

'Is someone accusing you of meddling?' Harry asked. 'It wouldn't be Amos by any chance, would it?'

'No, it would not!'

'Who then?'

'No one, yet.'

'Yet...?'

'It's October and Luca. I've been thinking.'

'Oh, dear.' Harry rolled his eyes and Petra slapped him on the arm.

'I need your help,' she said.

Harry shook his head. 'I'm not promising anything.'

'I'm going to play matchmaker,' she said.

'Again? You'll get a reputation, if you're not careful. And it didn't actually work, did it? If I remember rightly, Megan left Nathan's birthday party early because she was upset.'

'Only because she had fallen in love with him, and she felt she was betraying her husband. She came round in the end, though – Jeremy has been dead two years and it was time for her to move on with her life. Look at her and Nathan now!'

Harry ran a hand through his hair. 'I hope you know what you're doing,' he warned.

'October and Luca aren't speaking to each other, and she's handed her notice in. How much worse can it get? They'll thank me in the end.'

Amos wandered into the kitchen and placed his empty mug next to the sink. 'Who'll thank you?' he asked.

Petra put her tea towel down and leaned against the counter. 'I've got a plan to get October and Luca back together.' She ignored the quick exchange of glances between Harry and Amos. 'Amos, I need your help.'

He squinted at her. 'What do you need me to do?'

'Can you phone October and ask her to come to the stables to pick up the wages we owe her and her P45? Tell her to come after this evening's lesson. If she suggests coming up now, tell her I've got a little gift for her. You can tell her that you want to say goodbye to her, too,'

'What are you going to do?' Amos asked, and Harry groaned.

'Don't encourage her,' he said.

Petra grinned. 'I'm going to phone Luca and tell him we need to have a chat about Midnight. I'm going to ask him to call in after the lesson.'

'What if October's busy? Or Luca's got plans?' Harry argued.

'I'll just have to think of something else, won't I?'

Harry sighed loudly. 'I know I'm going to regret this, but you said you wanted my help?'

Petra rubbed her hands together. 'Yes, my love, I most certainly do.'

Luca could have done without driving to the stables this evening. It was dark and cold, and he wasn't in the mood. Surely whatever it was could have been discussed over the phone? But Petra had said she had to dash because she was about to take a lesson, and had ended the call before he'd been able to ask for clarification.

He'd been tempted to phone her back and tell her it would have to wait until tomorrow, or whenever he decided to return to the stables, but the one thing which made him decide to simply get it over with was her mention of teaching a lesson. If she was taking the class, it meant October wasn't. She'd have left for the day, so there was no chance of him bumping into her.

Feeling lost and rather sad, he drove up the lane, and was about to pull into the car park when he noticed there was tape across the entrance and a sign which said, "closed for resurfacing – please park around the back".

"Around the back" was where the horsebox, the trailer and the Land Rover lived. He didn't think the car park was too bad – if anything it was the lane which could do with new tarmac, but he obediently drove around the back of the stable block and switched the engine off.

Hoping the problem with Midnight wasn't a physical one, he headed for his horse's loose box first, to check on him, and was relieved to see the gelding contentedly chewing on the contents of his hay net.

'Hiya, big fella,' he murmured, slipping his hand into his pocket and bringing out a carrot.

Midnight whickered softly, and reached out to take it from him. Luca stroked him on the nose and the horse nudged him gently.

He sighed, and remained there for a moment, enjoying the contact, smelling the pleasant scent of dried grass and horse, and listening to the animal's crunching. Luca let his gaze roam over Midnight's back and down his legs, checking for any obvious signs that there was something wrong, but the horse seemed contented enough.

Scanning the inside of the stall and seeing that nothing appeared to be amiss, Lucas froze when he noticed a hair grip on a narrow ledge running around the top of the stable. A pang of regret and loss struck him as he pushed Midnight back, opened the door and went inside to retrieve it.

This was what October had been searching for the first time he'd met her, and as he held it his thoughts returned to that day. If he'd had known then what he knew now, he would have run a mile, because her betrayal hurt like hell.

He put the hair grip back. No doubt October would notice it soon enough. He was tempted to keep it as a reminder of her, even though she was lodged firmly in his mind and he guessed it would take a while to shift her. She'd burrowed her way under his skin more than he would have believed possible.

With a heavy sigh, he gave Midnight a final pat on the neck and walked towards the house to find Petra.

Harry watched Luca make his way across the yard towards the house, and felt idiotic as he skulked in the tack room, the door a tiny bit ajar to enable him to peep out.

The moment Petra opened the door and ushered Luca inside, Harry darted towards the car park, and hastily ripped the tape off and grabbed the cardboard sign, stuffing it behind a low-growing bush.

Only just in time, too, he thought in relief, as he heard another vehicle make its way up the lane. Petra had wanted to ensure that neither October nor Luca spotted the other's car in case one or the other of them buggered off before she had the chance to put her plan into action.

As Harry expected, the car belonged to October, and he slapped a sorrowful expression on his face and went to meet her.

'Sorry to hear you're leaving us,' he said, as she got out of her car. 'You fitted in brilliantly, I thought.'

'So did I, but... you know...' She shrugged.

'I've just about finished doing the rounds, so shall we go inside? It's a bit parky out here. Brrr.' He rubbed his hands together and blew on them.

'I would have come tomorrow, but Petra insisted on this evening. I'm going to miss this place.'

'Yes, well...' Harry coughed to cover his embarrassment. He'd never been good at subterfuge and he was certain she must realise there was something fishy going on. 'After you,' he said, gesturing towards the house.

And, as October walked ahead of him, he hoped Petra knew what she was doing.

October had barely stepped over the threshold when Queenie slammed into her legs uttering delighted little whimpers, and she bent down to stroke the dog's silky ears. Which was why she didn't notice Luca at first, but when she did, he looked as shocked as she felt.

'What are you doing here?' she demanded, shooting him an incredulous look. Her heart clenched and her stomach flipped over at the sight of him. She wanted desperately to throw herself into his arms and kiss him until he begged her to stop. But he'd made his position clear. He didn't want anything to do with her, and despite her swooping emotions she didn't think she wanted to be with a man who had so little trust in her.

'I thought you'd finished for the day,' he replied.

So he was only going to visit the stables when she wasn't here, was he? At least her resignation would solve that problem for him.

'I've finished for good,' she retorted. 'But **someone** wanted me to call in this evening to pick up my wages and P45.' She scowled at Petra. 'How could you? You know how I feel.'

'That's right, I do,' Petra replied. 'You two need to talk. Luca, you shouldn't believe everything you hear, and October, don't cut your nose off to spite your face. Please sort yourselves out, if not for your own sakes, then do it for mine. I need your help more than ever, October. Harry, Amos, let's leave them to it. And while we're at it, Amos, Harry and I have got something to tell you...'

October watched, open-mouthed, as Petra bustled her partner and her uncle out of the room. Then she turned to Luca and was about to tell him she was leaving when she saw his face.

'P45?' he asked.

'That's right.' She folded her arms and glared at him.

'Why? Do you think you'll stand a better chance of wrecking his marriage for good if you get a job closer to him?'

October seethed. 'You don't know what you're talking about.'

'I know what I heard.'

'You heard wrong,' she said, flatly. If Petra didn't return with her wages and her P45 soon, she was out of here. Petra could post it or drop it through her letterbox. She didn't need this aggro. 'Why are you here?'

'Isn't it obvious? I was conned.'

'As was I.' She threw her hands in the air. 'That's it, I'm off.'

She turned to leave but stopped when he said, 'What did Petra mean when she said I shouldn't believe everything I hear?'

October pulled a face. 'You heard half a conversation and jumped to the wrong conclusion. Then you didn't even have the decency to let me explain.'

'You can explain now.'

'I can't be bothered,' she retorted.

'Petra said you're not to cut your nose off to spite your face. Have I been a fool?'

'Sod Petra, and yes, you bloody well have!'

'Are you going to tell me what happened today with Zeus Fernsby, or not?'

October shuffled from foot to foot, wondering if it was worth explaining. Would it make any difference what Luca believed? Their relationship was over, practically before it had begun, so why should she waste her breath?

But she did, anyway. 'What you heard this morning was Zeus asking me to tell Minnow that a photo which had been taken of him with another woman, was me throwing myself at him because I was upset that it was over between us. If you'd stayed around long enough, you'd have heard me tell him to get lost.'

'He's been having an affair with someone else as well as you?'

'I'm not saying he was seeing her when he was with me – although he might have been. But even if he wasn't, he wasted no time in getting himself another mistress once I had been kicked into touch. You see, Zeus likes women with long, dark hair. He also likes his wife's money because he doesn't have a great deal of it himself. Here.' She took her phone out and showed him the photo.

It meant moving closer to him, and she was acutely aware of his cologne. It made her heady and breathless, and she struggled with the urge to wrap her arms around his neck and—

'It does look like you from the back,' he said, gazing at the screen. 'But it's not – your hair curls at the ends, and it's shinier. And your legs are longer.'

October stared up at him.

His lips were less than a foot away from hers.

She could almost taste him.

'I'm sorry.' His eyes met hers. 'I seem to make a habit of being a prat when you're around.'

'Are you sure you're not a prat all the time?' she replied, archly. Neither of them had moved.

'Probably. I'm sorry – I should have known better. You're nothing like the women I've dated in the past.'

'Glad to hear it.' She might sound sharp, but she certainly didn't feel it.

'Can you forgive me? Start over? Petra has gone to so much trouble...'

'You're incorrigible.'

'Is that a yes?'

'Yes.'

'Are you sure?'

'Shut up and kiss me,' October instructed.

And to her delight, Luca did as he was told.

Luca put his elbows on the table and steepled his chin on his clasped hands. 'Well?' he asked.

October swallowed her mouthful of wine and made a face.

'Don't you like it?' He'd splashed out and ordered one of the most expensive bottles the restaurant had. For her not to like it was a bit of a blow. He wanted to treat her to a fabulous meal because that's what one did on Valentine's Day, and the wine was part of the experience. As was the candle on the table, the oysters, the Lobster Thermador, and the soft music in the background. He'd even presented her with two dozen red roses when he'd picked her up in his car.

The restaurant itself was small and intimate, a perfect place for a night like tonight, and it was damned expensive.

'Have they got lemonade, do you think?' October asked, and his face fell until he realised she was joking. 'You didn't have to do all this, you know,' she said. 'I'd have been just as happy with lasagne and chips in the Black Horse.'

That was precisely why he wanted to treat her – because she didn't expect it or demand it. Luca wasn't rich by any stretch of the imagination, but he was quite well off and he hated it when his girlfriends in the past had felt aggrieved if he didn't take them to the most expensive places or lavish gifts on them.

October wasn't like that.

October was special – and he was incredibly thankful he'd found her.

He was also incredibly thankful that Petra had stuck her oar in the other evening, because if she hadn't he wouldn't be sitting here now gazing into the eyes of the loveliest woman on earth.

'Um, can I ask you a question?' he asked, his usual self-confidence hiding in the back row, scared to raise its head.

'You can. I mightn't answer you, though.'

'Now that you're working in the stables again and you've very graciously forgiven me—'

'Don't push it...'

'Do you think we can go steady? Boyfriend and girlfriend?'

'Excuse me, but I thought we already were!'

'Oh, I see. That's fantastic.' He'd hoped they were, but he'd had to ask, just to make sure. With October it wouldn't do to take anything for granted.

She grinned at him. 'It is, isn't it?' she said, and picked up her glass of rather expensive wine and drained it in one gulp.

Luca rolled his eyes, her irreverence towards the wine typical of her. She was exactly what he needed to keep him grounded.

She was exactly what he needed, full stop.

And as he stared into her eyes and saw his own love reflected back at him, he realised that physical possessions and money meant nothing when someone owned you body, heart and soul, the way October owned him.

Petra blew on her hands and walked into the kitchen, Queenie darting ahead of her. The dog's tail wagged furiously as she headed for Harry who was standing just inside the door.

He was looking anxious, and she realised why when he bent down to stroke the dog, and she could see beyond him.

'What's all this?' she asked, staring at the battered and well-worn kitchen table, which had been transformed with the aid of a pristine white tablecloth, a candle, a slender vase with a single red rose, and place settings for two.

'Valentine's Day,' Harry said.

Petra narrowed her eyes. 'Is that why Amos asked me to drive him into the village? I thought it was odd for him to visit Honeymead this evening.' Amos had suggested that she bring Queenie with her because several of the care home's residents wanted their fix of flop-eared spaniel. But he'd arranged to go for a drink in the Black Horse afterwards and didn't want to take the dog with him, arguing that Queenie would be better off at home. So Petra had waited whilst Queenie had said hello to everyone, and she'd then returned to the stables with the dog. It had meant she'd been out of the house for well over an hour.

'The pair of you can't be trusted,' Petra said.

'Don't you like it when the shoe is on the other foot?' Harry teased, going to the stove and stirring a saucepan. 'Amos is playing you at your own match-making game.'

'We don't need to be matchmaked – if that's a word. We're already together, if you hadn't noticed.'

'I'd noticed,' he said. 'Wash your hands and sit down. What do you want to drink?

I've got sparkling apple juice? Non-alcoholic beer?

'Apple juice, please.' Petra popped to the downstairs loo and washed her hands. Who knew Harry was such a romantic? She hadn't given Valentine's Day a single thought, and she wondered if she should have bought him a card.

Oh, well, too late for that now. At least he was cooking her a meal at home and not forcing her to go out to eat. She was so knackered these days, she didn't think she'd have been able to keep her eyes open.

The kitchen was full of delicious smells and her mouth watered as she sat down. Thankfully she'd not suffered from morning or any other time of day sickness, and she was looking forward to seeing what he'd cooked for her.

'Mmm, it looks yummy,' she said, when Harry put a plate in front of her. 'What is it?'

'Smoked salmon and pesto tartlet. Then there is steak with chilli butter, followed by salted caramel chocolate pots.'

'Wow. Did you make all this yourself?' She knew Harry could cook, but she didn't realise he could cook this well.

'Er, not really. I bought the tartlets, and the chilli butter. And I bought the chocolate pots. I'm cooking the steak from scratch, though.'

Petra laughed, filled to the brim with love for this wonderful man of hers. 'Have I told you recently how much I love you?'

'You have, but you can tell me again.' He smiled at her. 'Um, before you go all gooey on me, there's something I need to discuss with you. It's to do with the cowshed.'

'I honestly don't think we can go ahead with it, not now.' She glanced pointedly at her stomach. She was seventeen weeks pregnant already, and there wasn't enough time to do even a fraction of the work needed before the baby came – and that was assuming she was physically able to do it. 'It's a nice idea, but even if I wasn't expecting, there's no way we could afford the renovations.'

'What if we could?'

'But we can't, so there's no point in talking about it.' Petra put her fork down, her appetite fading. Why did Harry have to spoil what had been shaping up to be the most romantic meal she'd ever had, with talk of something that simply wasn't possible.

'The sale of the house in Cheltenham has been completed,' he said, beaming at her. 'I want to use my half to invest in the stables, starting with the renovations to the cowshed.'

'What? How? I mean, you can't do that!'

'Why not? It's **my** money. Timothy wants to see if he can buy the cottage he's renting with his share, and he'll ask Charity to move in with him. If he can do what he wants with his, why can't I do what I want with mine?'

'But, what about the risk?'

'What risk?'

Petra paused. How was she going to say this without sounding negative? She had every faith their relationship would last. But what if it didn't? There might be a very grey area indeed if they split up after he'd ploughed in his share of the money he'd made from the sale of the house which had originally belonged to his and Timothy's parents. She couldn't let him do it.

'What if we...you know...split up?' Her voice was small and timid. She hated to say it, but he'd pushed her into a corner.

'We're not going to split up,' he said firmly.

'How do you know?'

'I love you and you love me. Why should we split up? Besides, I want to marry you.' His eyes widened and his mouth fell open. 'Bugger, I didn't mean to ask you like that. Can I try again?'

'What?' Petra's brain was numb. Had she just heard him say he wanted to marry her?

She watched in astonishment as he slipped from his chair and got down on one knee. He put his hand in his pocket, brought out a small black velvet box, opened it and held it out to her.

'Petra, will you marry me?'

'What?' she repeated, her eyes on his hopeful face. She didn't look at the contents of the box.

'Will you do me the honour of being my wife?' He was smiling but there was a hint of strain in his voice.

'Is this about the baby? Because if it is, I don't want you to marry me just because I'm pregnant. Petra glared at him. She didn't want a pity marriage, or a doing-his-duty marriage. She wanted him to marry her because he loved her, not because he felt obliged to because she was carrying his child.

Harry lurched to his feet. 'Cramp,' he said, hopping about on one leg, whilst he tried to massage the calf on the other. If this wasn't so serious, Petra might have found it amusing.

'I am not asking you to marry me because you are pregnant,' he said through gritted teeth. 'I want you to be my wife because I love you, you silly woman. Ask Amos.'

Petra blinked in confusion. 'What's Amos got to do with it?'

'I asked him for your hand in marriage **before** I found out you were pregnant.' He shoved the box with the ring in it under her nose, forcing her to look at it.

'That's Aunt Mags's engagement ring!' she cried.

'It's yours now. I was taking it to the jewellers to be resized when I bumped into Cher.'

'You want me to marry you?'

'For god's sake woman, that's what I've been trying to tell you for the past five minutes. Now, do you want to be my wife or not?'

Petra raised her eyebrows. 'Since you put it so nicely, how can I say no?'

'You're saying yes?'

She nodded.

Harry snapped the lid of the box shut and danced around the room. 'She said yes, she said yes!'

'Harry?'

Harry stopped leaping about. 'What?'

'Are you going to ask me properly and get down on one knee?'

Harry pursed his lips. 'You are so annoying.' He walked towards the table and gingerly lowered himself onto one knee, wincing as he did so.

'But you love me anyway,' she said, holding out the third finger of her left hand for him to slip the ring on it.

'I must be mad, but I love you to the moon and back, and our little one,' he said, placing his palm on her stomach.

'That's good, because you're stuck with us now. If you try to get out of it, Amos will come after you.'

'I'll never want to get out of it. You're my whole world.'

'I love you too, Harry. More than you'll ever know. Now, please can you get up so I can finish my tartlet – I'm starving!'

'Here I am trying to be all romantic and all you can think about is food,' he grumbled, using the table to pull himself up.

'I **am** eating for two,' Petra retorted primly, but the adoration on Harry's face when he looked at her took her breath away.

Maybe the tartlet could wait after all…

The Stables on Muddypuddle Lane Series

Spring

Summer

Autumn

Winter

Valentine Kisses

The Patter of Tiny Feet

Wedding Bells

Christmas

About Etti

Etti Summers is the author of wonderfully romantic fiction with happy ever afters guaranteed.

She is also a wife, a mum, a pink gin enthusiast, a veggie grower and a keen reader.

www.ingramcontent.com/pod-product-compliance
Lightning Source LLC
Chambersburg PA
CBHW020749190726
48285CB00006B/1947